MW01125018

VINCE
&
ELLE

WILLOW WINTERS
WALL STREET JOURNAL & USA TODAY BESTSELLING AUTHOR

I was innocent before him, and he wanted nothing more than to ruin me. And if I'm honest, I wanted him too, even knowing I shouldn't.

I knew he was a bad man, it doesn't take more than a single look to know it. Dark eyes and a charming smile that's made to fool girls like me.

Still, I caved; I gave into temptation.

And then I saw something I shouldn't have. Wrong place, wrong time. The mafia doesn't let witnesses simply walk away.

Regret has a name, and it's Vincent Valetti.

He won't let them kill me, but he's not going to let me go either.

HIS
HOSTAGE

PROLOGUE

Elle

I already regret this. I walk farther into the office as he shuts the door with a loud click. Everyone must've seen me walk back here with him and they're going to know what we're doing. I feel like a cheap whore. His hands wrap around my waist and pull my ass into him. His hard erection digs into my back. My core heats as he leaves an open-mouthed kiss on my neck. His hot breath runs chills down my body, and I cave. I *need* this. My body molds to his, and my hands reach behind me and around his neck. My fingers tangle in his hair. I don't care what they think. For once, I just want to feel good.

Vince

Good girl. I knew if I just got her alone I'd be able to loosen her up. She's in need, and I know exactly what to

do. My fingers tease her skin as I pull the camisole over her head. I have to pull away for a moment, and she takes the chance to turn around. She stands on her tiptoes to crush her lips against mine. I part her lips with my tongue and taste her, sucking on her bottom lip while I unhook her bra. I break away, and drop to my knees to unbuckle her shorts and pull them down. Lace panties. They'll be easy to tear right off.

My breathing is loud, nearly frantic, and my heart beats wildly in my chest. I can't believe I'm doing this. He tears through my panties with his thumbs and tosses them carelessly to the side, not taking his eyes off me. Another wave of arousal soaks my core as I clench my thighs. He grins and grips my hips, forcing my pussy into his face while he breathes in deep. I'd die of embarrassment, but his loud groan and languid lick make my eyes close, and my mouth part in ecstasy. He stands up and pulls my bra off of me, and the straps tickle my arms as I watch his eyes focus on my breasts. My nipples harden under his lust-filled gaze.

So fucking hot. I knew she was beautiful, but damn, I have to take a moment to appreciate just how gorgeous she is. I grip her thighs and lift her up so I can put her ass on the edge of the desk. I lean down and suck her hardened, pale pink nipple into my mouth. Her head falls back, and a soft moan falls from her lips.

He pulls back and lets my nipple pop out of his mouth before getting onto his knees. Holy shit. He's gonna go down on me. My breath stills in my lungs and I try to close my legs from mortification, but his hands on my inner knees stop them and he pushes me wide open to stare at my pussy. My cheeks flame and I can't look because I'm so fucking horrified.

"You want me to stop, sweetheart?" I know she doesn't. I bet she's never been taken care of like this before. She's in for a treat. She bites her lip and shakes her head. I smile at her, and then focus my attention back to her needy, delicious cunt. Her pussy lips are glistening with arousal and I fucking love it. I lean down and take a long lick from her entrance to the clit. So sweet. I flick her throbbing clit with my tongue and she finally relaxes under me. I smile into her heat and grip her ass tight, angling her into a position that's good for me.

Oh my god. It feels so good. I have to focus on staying quiet. My teeth dig into my bottom lip as I shamelessly rock my pussy into his face. His tongue massages against my clit as his fingers dip into me and curl, hitting my G-spot and making my back arch. Holy fuck!

She's loving what I'm doing; her body is so damn responsive, just like I knew she would be. I can't wait to get into that pussy and watch those tits bounce. They aren't the biggest breasts I've ever seen, but they're perky and fit in

my hands just right. I bite down on her clit, not hard, just enough to send her over the edge as her pussy clamps down on my fingers. She's so fucking tight. Her pussy is going to feel like heaven on my dick.

My thighs squeeze around his head. I want to stop, but I can't control my body. A cold sweat breaks out along my skin and I feel paralyzed as my body ignites with waves of pleasure.

Her arousal soaks my hand. I keep my fingers in that tight cunt, stroking her front wall and sucking her clit to get every bit of her orgasm out. I don't stop until she's lying limp on the table. I smile and gently place a hand on her trembling thigh. That should calm her ass down.

That pussy's soft, hot, and wet. And waiting to be filled. I unzip my jeans and let them drop to the floor while I stroke my cock. It's begging to be wrapped in her heat.

The sound of his zipper makes my eyes pop open and pulls me from my sated daze. Oh fuck! My heart pounds in my chest, and my breathing comes in shallow pants. I push the hair out of my face and swallow thickly. I'm going to lose my virginity. I don't want it to happen this way.

She props herself up and closes her legs. My brow furrows with confusion and my body heats with anger. What the fuck is she doing? She leaving me high and dry? That'd be a fucking first. I know she enjoyed me feasting

on her pussy. She'll fucking love what I can do to her while she's impaled on my dick.

I clear my throat and nervously try to reach his gaze. A violent blush reaches my cheeks and burns my chest. I just don't want it like this. My pussy is begging to let him fuck me, and my dark fantasies want to come to life. I want him to take me and pound into me until I'm screaming. But I can't pull the trigger.

"You all right, sweetheart?" His question holds a hint of admonishment. My mind goes wild with the thought of him holding me down and fucking me exactly how he wants. Punishing me for refusing him. But I don't want to refuse him. I want to give him pleasure, too. I bite my bottom lip to steady the need to tremble. I scoot to the edge of the desk and drop easily to my knees.

She immediately takes me into her inviting mouth and sucks the head of my dick. I groan and let my head fall back and spear my fingers through her hair, putting easy pressure on the back of her head. Her hot, eager mouth feels so fucking good. She takes me in deeper and massages her tongue along the underside of my dick. Her head bobs on my cock and her cheeks hollow out from how hard she's sucking. I let her go at her own pace, but I really want to shove myself down her throat. I hold back though. She wouldn't like the things I wanna do to her.

A sick fantasy of him skull-fucking me flashes before my eyes, and I find myself taking him deeper than I'm able, trying to choke myself on his dick. My throat closes around his thick length and he pumps his hips in short, shallow thrusts. I pull back and breathe quickly while his hands clench into fists in my hair. As soon as I have air I take him in my mouth and do it again.

She's acting like she fucking loves this. She pulls off again and licks the underside of my dick, stroking me with her hand while she licks my length. Her wide, blue eyes stare up at me. She's looking for approval. "Baby, you keep doing that, and I'm gonna cum." Just watching her, my balls draw up and my spine tingles, but I hold back the urge to cum. I'm not done with her yet.

I've never done this before, but I've read so many romance novels and articles... and watched so much porn. I know I need to shove him deep into my throat and swallow. I do it again and choke a little, but as soon as I can, I work him into the very back of my throat until I can't breathe at all. My hands rest at my thighs. I want to massage his balls, or push against his taint searching for that little spot I read about that's supposed to make a man go off, but instead I dig my fingers into my thighs. I pull back and take a deep breath. I feel spit drip down my chin and I quickly wipe it away.

She's too fucking good. I want in that hot pussy, but it's

not going to happen. "Baby, I'm gonna cum." I get ready to pull away; I'm sure she's not the type of girl who's gonna want to swallow. Although, I didn't peg her to be so good at giving head either. The idea that's she's had practice pisses me off. I don't get jealous, but I don't fucking like that idea. Then my sweetheart does the sexiest fucking thing. She closes her eyes, sticks her tongue out flat under the head of my dick and pushes her breasts together.

I open my eyes when I hear the sexiest groan I've ever heard and feel his hot cum on my breasts. I watch as waves splash against my breasts and it gives me the deepest satisfaction. I smile shyly and calm my breathing. I did this to him.

I open my eyes and see her cute little smirk. "Lick it clean, sweetheart." My dick's still hard as her tongue darts out to lap up the bit of sticky cum left on my dick. She sits back on her heels, far more relaxed than she was before, and then she reaches for her clothes. I frown, and my heart drops a little in my chest. She's ready to leave? Already?

I feel a little sick knowing he's gonna want me out of here now that our little fling is over. Only a little though. That's what I'm telling myself, at least. I feel so dirty, but I love it. I watch in my periphery as he leans over the desk and then hands me some tissues to wipe off my chest. I give him a tight smile and quickly clean myself off. I want it again, but I don't think he's the type of guy that sticks with one girl. And I'm not going to give myself to someone who isn't going to want me after. I don't know what I was thinking. Regret starts to consume me, but I shake it off. I wanted this. I got exactly what I wanted.

"You got a lot of studying to do?" I ask, as I pull up my boxers and jeans. I know she's in a rush to get out, but I'll at least stay with her while she's out there. I'm sure they know we were back here fooling around, but I want them to give her the respect she deserves. I'm not gonna leave her for them to stare down and judge.

No way I'm staying here. I spot my bag sitting next to the door. I'll just sneak out the back. I shake my head at his question. "I'm pretty tired. I'm just gonna head home." The high I felt just moments ago is already waning, and I'm feeling more and more uncomfortable as I stand and adjust my shorts. I have no clue where my panties are. Not that it really matters since he destroyed them.

My eyes close as the denim push against my sensitive clit. Damn, I want him again. I want him inside of me. But not like this. I'm not going to lose my virginity like this. Not to someone I don't even know. The thought makes my gaze drop to the floor, and I try to swallow the shame creeping up on me.

Shit, I can see the regret. I don't fucking want that. I wanna see this girl again. I *need* to have her cumming on my dick. I barely got a taste of her. "I'll drive you home, sweetheart."

I bite my bottom lip and grip the straps of my tote. I put it on my shoulder and nod. I wince as the straps bite down on my tender skin. Fucking hell, why'd I pack so damn much and walk the entire way here? He's quick to reach out and take it from me. It's a sweet gesture, and I don't expect it. I assume he's hoping to get into my pants when he drops me off. That sure as shit is not going to happen. I think about what's waiting for me at home and get all pissed off. I can't fucking believe how shitty my life has become. The reminder makes me close my eyes, and I try to will away the anger.

I don't like wherever her head has gone. Gently, I place my hand on her shoulder and squeeze slightly. "Stop it, Elle." Her eyes shoot up at me with daggers as she shoves my hand away.

"Just because we just did that," I say with anger as I motion to the desk, "does not mean that you have any right to tell me what to do." Immediately I regret my outburst. It's not his fault. Shit. I ruined this. Whatever this is. Was. Whatever, it's over with now.

What the fuck has gotten into her? I have half a mind to throw her ass on the desk and fuck that snarky attitude right out of her. I know just how to do it, too. Deep and slow. I'd fucking torture the orgasms from her until she quits being like this. So damn defensive.

This was such a fucking mistake. I swing the door open

and walk out as quickly as I can, leaving him behind. I keep walking, past the opening for the dining room of the bistro and straight ahead. There's got to be a door to get the fuck out of here where no one will see me. I twist the knob to what I think will be an exit and push the heavy door open.

I finally get a grip and go after her, determined to have her smart little mouth wrapped around my cock again. I take one step out of the office and bolt after her. Not that room! What the fuck is she doing?

Holy fuck! I gasp as my eyes widen at what I'm seeing, and instinctively take a step backwards, but my back hits a brick wall of muscle. Strong arms wrap around my waist and face, and a hand covers my mouth to mute the scream that's ripped from my throat.

God damn it. I can't believe this is happening. I hold her tight to me as she struggles in my grasp. I can't fucking believe she walked back here. Tommy and Anthony are staring back at me with looks of outrage.

I try to scream. I try to pull away. I need to do something, anything. Tears burn my eyes and my body heats, then goes numb with fear. Fuck! It's useless. He won't let me go. "Please!" I try to scream, but his hand stays clamped over my mouth. Tears fall helplessly down my heated cheeks as my body racks with sobs.

I wish I could let her go, but if I do, I know the family will have to get rid of her.

If he'd just let me go, I wouldn't say anything.

She'd swear up and down not to talk, but it wouldn't be enough.

I'll plead with him, he has to believe me. I try to speak, but his hand pushes harder against my lips.

I wish I could believe her, but there's no way I can risk it. I tilt my head to the door, letting them know I'm taking her away.

My feet drag and stumble as he pulls me back into the office. I'll offer him anything. There has to be some way to convince him.

She hardly struggles against me as I close the door. I don't think there's any way I could convince the *familia* to let her go. Maybe there's a way.

I'm going to have to keep her until they're convinced.
She's my hostage now.

CHAPTER 1

ELLE

EARLIER THAT DAY

I shift my weight and groan. This bag is freaking killing my shoulder. I don't know why I packed so many textbooks. I shoved all three in to my bag along with my laptop before I took off. Barely 15 minutes later, the straps are digging into my skin, making it feel raw and destroying my resolve to study. Part of me just wants to drop the bag and go to a bar. I'm so fucking pissed off. I shake off the bitter resentment and walk a little faster. I shouldn't have brought so much grad work. It's not like I'm in any mood to do it anyway. Not after fighting with my mother *again*.

I wish I didn't have to pay her fucking bills, so I could move back to my shitty little apartment. Her poor decisions keep fucking me over. I can't afford to live anywhere but with her now. Why the hell did she get a mortgage? Did she have to fuck me over like that? She had to know she couldn't afford it. I told her not to do it. I *knew* this would happen. And now I'm stuck here helping her ass out *again*, while she gets sober ... *again*.

I'm tired of sacrificing everything for her, but I just can't say no. I can't abandon her. Even if it's draining the life out of me. I'm just lucky I was able to transfer to a local university so I could move back in with her. I need to get my shit together so I don't fail. Playing catch-up is a bitch though. And I'm struggling to find the motivation.

I leave for not even three months and she ups and moves for some loser she met online. And then buys a house for *both* of them. I shake my head and bite the inside of my cheek while tears burn my eyes. I won't cry again. I push them back and concentrate on the anger. Mom has so many problems. It's fucked up.

I don't care that she thinks he's going to change and pay her back all the money that he squandered. It's not fucking acceptable. I don't trust this guy, just like I didn't trust the last, but does she listen to me? No. Not unless I'm rattling off my bank account number.

I know I saw a little place down the street on the way in that looked like a good spot to park my ass and attempt to relax. I just need to get out of that house so I can study without being so pissed. I groan and swing the tote over my shoulder to try to ease the pressure of the weight. After a few minutes of walking I calm down and smirk, remembering what bag I picked for today. The text on the tote reads, "My book club only reads wine labels." A smile grows on my face and I can't help it. I may have a completely new life now, a really shitty one, but at least I still have my old sense of humor.

After a few minutes I nearly consider turning back to get my car, but then I pick up the pace remembering that asshole is still there. She'd better kick his ass out. I told her I'm not going to help out financially if he's there. My fists clench harder as a long, strangled breath leaves me. Her words ring in my ear. "But you're on the mortgage!" She's such a bitch. And technically, a criminal for forging my name. But am I going to do anything about it? Nope. I always keep my mouth shut and do what's best. At least what's best for others. I don't even know what's best for me anymore.

I clench my jaw, and feel anger rising inside of me. It's not fucking right to be angry at her. Or is it? I just wish she were more responsible. I wish she weren't a fucking alcoholic. Why do I feel so remorseful for hating that she puts me through this? More than anything else, I feel guilty, like her being so unhappy is all my fault.

The place I saw on the drive to the house, Valetti's Italian Bistro, is just another block away. Hopefully they'll have some booth in the back that's empty. And alcohol. I could really use a drink. It's a little late for dinner, so maybe it'll be deserted and I can get my studying done in peace. I walk up the brick paved walkway and admire how rustic the place looks before opening the front door. This entire area has a small-town feel. I like it.

I'd like it more if I wasn't forced to be here though. As soon as I'm done with graduate school, I'm gone. I'll give Mom an allowance, maybe, and leave to find a place like this that isn't tainted. A nice, small town with family-owned restaurants just like this. I smile and let out an easy sigh. Everything's going to be alright. I just have to push through everything and work a little harder. And figure out a way to stop being a freaking enabler.

I take a quick glance around the place. It's dark for a restaurant, with a few dim lights placed symmetrically around the dining area. The walls are a soft cream, and the chairs and booths are a deep red. It's just my style. A little grin forms on my face as I spot an empty booth in the back on the right. It's directly across from another booth in the narrow room, almost like they belong to each other, but there's an obvious separation. I take quick strides to claim it.

I scoot into the seat and let the back of my tote hit the cushion before sliding the straps off my arm. Holy hell, that feels so much better. I rub my shoulder and look down to see two angry red marks from the straps. My lips purse. Next time I'm just bringing the laptop and my notes. And my car.

I lick my lips and pull out my laptop to bring up the syllabus. I downloaded it before I left, but I'm hoping this place has Wi-Fi. I breathe in deep and click to see. It's password protected. Damn. I don't like that. That means I have to talk to someone. And I really don't like that. I prefer to keep to myself. My eyes look past the brightly lit screen and search the place for a waitress, but there isn't one readily apparent. My shoulders sag with disappointment. Where the hell is the waitress? My eyes drift to directly in front of me and catch the gaze of one of the men sitting across the aisle in the opposite booth.

I quickly break eye contact, but I got a good enough look at him that heat and moisture pool in my core. He's fucking hot. Dark hair that's long enough to grab, and dark, piercing eyes to match. His tanned skin and high cheekbones are emphasized by the dim lighting.

I swallow thickly and hope the heat in my cheeks isn't showing as a violent red blush on my face. My eyes hesitantly look back at the man in question, and judging from the smirk on his face, he did see. Shit! I rest my left elbow on the table and attempt to casually cover my face while searching again for a waitress. I'm gonna need a drink to calm these nerves and focus on my work.

"Would you like a menu?" I turn to see a young man, very Italian-looking, with olive skin and bright green eyes waiting for my response. He seems nice enough and obviously still in high school.

"No thanks, just a drink please?"

"What can I get you?" he asks, and then gives me a forced smile. *Well, damn. I'm sorry me being here has rained on your parade.* I shake off the snide inner remark. Maybe he's just had a rough day. Like me.

"Citrus vodka and Sprite, please." *My favorite.* I smile brightly at him, hoping maybe a little sunshine will rub off on him, but it's a no-go. He gives me the same tight smile with a short nod, and leaves.

This place is odd. I never would've guessed that guy was a waiter. He was only wearing black jeans and a black tee. It's not the uniform I'd expect from a nice place like this. Or the service. A small, self-conscious part of me thinks maybe it's me. Maybe they don't like that I've come in here just to drink and study. There's a long bar on the other side of the room though. I close my eyes and shake my head slightly. It's not me. I'm always thinking that. I need to stop that. It's a bad habit.

I stretch out my shoulders and look back at the computer screen. I mumble a curse under my breath. The guy across the aisle distracted me, and I didn't even get to ask for the password when the waiter finally came around. Damn, I'll have to remember to ask when he comes back with my drink. I click my tongue on the roof of my mouth. He didn't even ask for ID. I wonder if I'm starting to look old. I purse my lips as I consider this thought. No fucking way. He's just a shit waiter.

Satisfied with that, I return to my syllabus and pull out the corresponding textbook and a yellow highlighter. I've got three chapters from this one to highlight, and then I'll write my notes down. I nod my head. That's a good plan. I may have transferred schools two years into my PhD, but I should be able to bang out all three classes this semester and be back on track. I've got Molecular and Cell Biology up first. I cringe a bit. It's all just so much fucking memorizing that I'll never ever use again. This may be a long fucking study hour. Correction. Hours.

My heart sinks in my chest at the thought of wasting the night like this. I'm so tired of late nights in the lab or studying. I've alienated everyone in my life. My "social life" consists of bailing my mom out of jail and talking to my primary investigator about our research. I don't even want to pursue the summer internship I was offered. I thought I'd love doing cancer research, but my only choices at this point are working with either cells or animals. And neither one is tempting. I have no clue why I'm still working my ass off for this. But if I let it go, what do I have left? Without my career, I've merely wasted years of my life hiding from reality. The thought depresses me to the core.

"Whatcha doing, sweetheart?" My body jolts as I hear the question, and I turn my head to stare at the Italian Stallion that sneaked up on me.

Hearing his masculine voice and watching his corded

muscles ripple as he moves to sit across from me in my booth brings back that initial desire, full fucking force. My pussy heats and I clench my thighs. Holy hell. His muscles are rock fucking hard, and there isn't an ounce of fat on his body. His dark eyes pierce into me. I break away from his gaze and curse my hormones for making me so horny. Not fucking fair. I feel a deep urge to just fuck my frustrations away.

I don't need sex. 've never had it, never done the dirty deed, but no one *needs* sex. I bite my lip and feel my shoulders turn inward as doubt creeps in. How the hell would I know if it would help? I've never had the courage to go through with it.

I can't believe he's sitting with me, but at the same time, I don't want to be hit on. I'm sure he's just trying to get lucky. I don't have time for this. I have to catch up on my studying so I don't fall behind even more. But I find my eyes drifting down his body the way I imagine his would trail down mine. His white tee shirt is pulled taut over his muscles. My eyes dart to meet his as I belatedly realize that I'm blatantly staring. A blush blazes in my cheeks, and my stomach drops.

I nervously tuck my hair back behind my ears and lick my lips. I drop my eyes, and focus steadily on the white tablecloth for a moment. I clear my throat and gather the courage to look Mr. Hunk in the eyes. "I have to study." I'm surprised I had the courage to say anything at all, and that my voice was mostly steady. I wish I weren't so dismissive though. It came out a bit shorter than I would have liked. I don't want him to think I'm some bitch. It's not that. I'm just awkward, and I really do need to study.

"What's your name?" he asks.

"Elle," I respond quickly, and try to keep my voice steady. But it yelps slightly because of my nerves. Fuck! I sound like a damn squeaky mouse. I am a grown woman, damn it! I clear my throat again and wish my drink were here. My hair cascades down from behind my ears, and I nervously reach up to tuck it back into place and take a breath.

This is a bad idea. I'm not stupid; I need to stop this shit. He's trouble with a capital T, and I'm not in any position to handle him.

"I'm Vince. What are you studying, sweetheart?"

Vince. I like that name. It suits him well.

I consider answering him, but he just wants into my pants. And I need to study. I know this, yet I can't help getting so wound up and hot for him. All fucking week I've been miserable. Hating my life. Hating how I let my mother pressure me into giving up everything I had going for me so I can be her rock. Just like she always fucking does. I haven't done one thing for myself in so long. Not one reckless thing *ever* that I can think of. Nothing I wanted to do purely out of desire.

Would it be so bad? Would it really be so wrong to just flirt a bit? Flirting. My lips press into a line. I don't even know how to flirt. So yeah, it would be a bad idea.

CHAPTER 2

VINCE

I'm so fucking bored. I haven't done a damn thing all day. I sit back in my seat at the bistro and stretch my legs. I love sitting here at the booth – at my booth – just relaxing. But only when I've earned it. Today, I haven't earned a damn thing. I may need to run by the shipping docks to make sure everything is set up to run smoothly, but other than that, my to-do list is short. I pull out my iPhone from my jeans and sigh. I can at least check the stocks.

Joe leans over to look at my phone and laughs. "Thought you were checking out those nude pics again, not that stupid shit." I smirk at him, not bothering to give a verbal response, and get back to my portfolio.

First off, Leah's pictures are no longer on my phone. And they never should've been there. Fucking nosy prick saw them the second they came through. I deleted them without even looking, but he hasn't forgotten.

She knew it was only for one night. Desperation doesn't look good on anyone, and I'm not the kind of guy who commits. I frown, thinking about how she should have more respect for herself. I told her I didn't want a relationship. It was a quick, dirty fuck and that's it. It was months ago. Thank fuck she finally let it go and moved on to someone else.

Secondly, my portfolio isn't stupid shit. It's a moneymaker. A real fucking good moneymaker that rivals what I get from the *familia*. But Joe's not gonna get that. Most of these guys will never understand. They don't want any responsibility, or have any ambition. They want easy work where they don't have to learn a damn thing, just listen to orders. And that's why I'm the underboss, and not any of them. If you're not hungry for success, you'll never get it.

A grin grows across my face as I watch the door open and see a beautiful blonde walk in like she belongs here. This is a small town, but she's not someone I've seen around town before. I let my eyes drift down her body in absolute appreciation. She's wearing a thin, cream colored camisole and tight jean shorts. There's a sweet innocence radiating from her. Her waist is narrow, but her hips are wide. She's got one hell of a cute little pear-shaped body. It's a body that could take a punishing fuck. My dick hardens just thinking about gripping onto those hips.

I readjust my cock and take a look around the room. The other guys notice, but they don't show it. It's only us and the sweet little blonde here now. Technically this restaurant is a public place. People come here to get an inside look, but it's not like we'd actually do some shit here. We hardly even use the freezer room anymore. Hardly. There's some shit going on in the back room right now, and that's why I'm forced to sit here and make sure it doesn't get out of hand. It's not as if my cousins can't handle the job on their own. I know they can. But I have to wait here till they're done.

She smiles looking around the room, and her eyes light up as she quickly strides to take a seat across from me. It prompts a small chuckle from me. She obviously takes delight in the little things. I like that.

The people in this town don't come in that often anymore. They know my Pops is Don. Everyone *knows* it, but no one can prove it. I look to my left and see Joe smile as he watches the sweet little blonde scoot into the booth across from us. Joe can back the fuck off, that pussy is mine.

I grin at her being so damn cute and shy. She obviously has no idea that she's walked into the mafia headquarters. A low, deep chuckle vibrates my chest as she blushes and covers her face. Sweet. She's a definite sweetheart; I like it. *Sweetheart.*

She's looking around like a waitress is gonna come and

give her a menu. I look over to Brant. He knows the drill. He should be getting his ass up and playing the part. It takes a minute for him to put down his phone and walk over to her with a forced smile. Little shit. He's only 17 and doesn't do much for the family, for obvious reasons. He should be thrilled to wait on a woman like that. Maybe the prick's hormones haven't hit him yet.

I give her a minute to get adjusted. I nearly laugh when I see her disappointed expression viewing the laptop screen and then watch her eyes search the room. She's upset about the Wi-Fi. How freaking cute. I can practically hear her every thought. She's so easy to read. So expressive. I bet she'd be that way in bed, too.

At that thought, I stand up and walk over to her. No time like the present. I know I'm going to be interrupting, but I don't wait. I'm an impatient prick. When I want something, I go for it. And I sure as fuck want her.

"Whatcha doing here, sweetheart?" My little prey jumps upright and her hand flies to her chest. I restrain myself from laughing and slip into the seat across from her, watching her face to make sure I'm welcome. She smiles slightly, and that beautiful blush rises to her cheeks again. She gives off an innocent vibe that makes me want to test her. My arm rests on the back of the booth, but it's a good distance away from her. I don't want to come on too strong. Not yet.

I'm surprised my sweetheart isn't drooling. She obviously

likes what she sees. Which makes me real fucking happy, and more eager than I should be to get into her pants. It's been a while, but the need to fuck her senseless is riding me hard. Her pouty lips beg me to nibble them. I can practically hear her panting while I rut between her legs. Her chest rises and falls as her eyes find mine, and a look of embarrassment crosses her face. She shouldn't be embarrassed, not at all. She's obviously a woman with needs. I could take care of those for her. It'd be my fucking pleasure.

"I have to study." She looks nervous, like I'm about to devour her. She's smart, 'cause that's exactly what I'm going to do. It's obvious that she's a good girl who knows better. But I've learned that good girls happen to love bad boys. And that's exactly who I am, so she's in for a treat.

"What's your name?" I ask, completely ignoring her statement.

"Elle." She's quick to respond. I like that.

"I'm Vince. What are you studying, sweetheart?" I deliberately lick my bottom lip and watch her eyes dart to my mouth as her own lips part slightly. I know how to play this game. It's exactly the kind of game that hard to get types like to play. Although, I don't have to play it often. And she doesn't really come off as that kind of girl.

I pick up her textbook and my brow furrows when I see the cover. She's really fucking smart. "Biology?" I keep my voice even as I set the book back down. My confidence takes a small hit though. She's a good girl, and she's in school. Judging from the book, she's taking some pretty fucking hard classes. I never went that road. Not like my brother Dom. I mean, I still know my shit. I never wanted to sit in class and try to be the teacher's pet. But I'm damn sure this broad isn't wanting a man like me.

She's not going to want the bad boy who's only going to derail her plans. At most, maybe she'd consider me someone to go slumming with. But my read on her isn't giving me that vibe; she's not the kind of woman who'd go to a dive looking for a dirty fuck to get her off, the later tell her girlfriends what she did. Her soft blue eyes stare back at me with lust, but she's holding herself back. I can tell. And I'm finding the challenge alluring.

"Yup! Bio." Her voice squeaks a little and it makes me grin. I love that I'm getting to her. I can tell she thinks this is a bad idea, and she's right. Just like I thought, smart girl. "I--" She starts to speak, but I cut her off.

"You want to be a biologist, or a teacher?" I ask her, knowing she'd be too polite to talk over me. She blinks a few times, proving me right. "I just ask 'cause my brother went to school, but he decided to teach." I take a deep breath, then sit back in my seat as I run a hand through my hair. "Seems like a shit deal, though. That degree cost a lot, but teaching doesn't pay dick."

My jaw tics as I realize I let a bit of profanity slip. I don't know why it bothers me. It's who I am, and this is how I talk. All I'm looking for is a quick fuck, and I think she'd enjoy my filthy mouth. Or at the very least, she'd enjoy it on her pussy. But something about cussing in front of her seems off. She's too sweet to taint.

"I have no fucking clue, to be honest," she says, and I smirk at her response. I love her blasé attitude and that her sweet little mouth can say naughty things. I've always wondered why people spend so much of their lives doing things that don't thrill them. I need the high I get from my line of work. I don't get people who work themselves to the bone for something their heart isn't into.

"Then why do it?" I ask, and I honestly want to know. Her hesitation makes me think she doesn't know how to answer. Then her eyes fall to the table, and her lips tug down into a frown.

Damn. That's not what I was expecting. I feel like an asshole for putting that sad look on her face. "Didn't mean to upset you, sweetheart." She shakes her head and looks back at me with a pained expression. She swallows and takes a deep breath. She's so easy to read, and the only thing coming off of her right now is sorrow. I don't like it. It's not the read I got on her when she walked in.

"I'm just tired," she says. Her lips press into a sad smile. It's a lie. She may be tired, but that's not what's eating her. This is where I usually steer the conversation back to the direction of my dick, or just leave. But the fucking words come out of my unfiltered mouth with concern. "Tell me what's wrong," I say imperiously. I demand, rather than ask her for an answer, because I don't want to give her the option not to confide in me. I want to know. Some sick, twisted part of me feels like I could fix it all.

Her eyes narrow like she doesn't want me prying. I get that. To be honest, I'm surprised the question popped out of my mouth. Finally, she answers, "I'm just not happy with the decisions I've made for people who don't appreciate them." Vague answer, but a bit of relief washes over her. Like she's happy just to get it off her chest. Surprisingly enough, she continues opening up.

"I keep moving my life around for my mother, who only seems to date shitty assholes who take, take, take until she's spent. And then she runs to me when she has nothing."

My heart fucking hurts for this broad. She's intelligent, beautiful, and sweet, yet she's hurting like this over her own mother? That's a damn shame. "Why do you do it?" I ask her. I sure as shit wouldn't. Not that Ma would ever put me in that position.

She shakes her head and just like that, the walls come up. My fingers itch to touch her. I want to soothe that bit of sadness. I've never felt something like this before, like I could make her life better. Like I *want* to make her life better. It makes me feel uneasy. But I can't fucking stop it.

"Because she's my mother." She gives me a tight smile and reaches for the drink I didn't even see on the table. At least Brant's good at keeping a low profile.

I'm really out of my fucking element here. I'm an expert on getting laid, but this sure as shit isn't it.

I raise my eyebrows and take a deep breath. "I can see wanting to help your mom, I guess." I should give her some time to study and get out of this shit mood. "You want me to leave you alone so you can study?"

I feel like an ass, asking like a little bitch. I'd rather she didn't waste her time doing shit that makes her unhappy when I could have her bent over moaning in ecstasy. I should just drag her to the back room and give her what she needs. My dick is so fucking hard for her. I haven't had any ass for a while now, and the barest hint of her breasts is peeking out through her tank top, taunting me.

But, if she wants to bury herself in her work to forget about that shit, I can wait until she's done and then make sure she gets what she really needs. That, and I know she can read me like the back of her hand. She's smart. If I pull a move now, then she'll know what's up and just push me away. If I give her this, there's a better chance of me getting that ass later. I can wait. Usually I don't have to, but I'm willing to deal with a bit of blue balls, for a little while at least.

"Yeah, thanks. Sorry to be such a downer." Her words drip with disappointment and sarcasm. What the hell? She's blowing me off? Nope, not gonna fucking happen. I look like a bad influence, because I am a bad influence. It's real cute that she thinks I'll just go ahead and leave her to do her work after that smartass answer. I'm not that kind of guy though.

"I don't like the way you talk about yourself," I say with a hard edge to my voice, because I really don't fucking like it. Being honest and open like that takes courage, at the very least. She shouldn't be putting herself down. I also don't like her attitude, not one fucking bit. She's pushing me.

She squares her shoulders and looks me straight in the eyes. She speaks calmly, but her voice is strong. "I can do what I'd like." Her defiance makes my dick hard, and I ache to turn her over right here in front of everyone and show her what a good punishing fuck she needs right now. Then she adds, "And right now I'd like to study." With my blood boiling and my agitation growing, she grinds her teeth and turns her shoulder to me, effectively dismissing me.

"You could really use a release, sweetheart." I can't stop myself from saying it. I shouldn't. I should let her finish her work, and I sure as shit shouldn't get involved with her problems. But her being so short and snippy with me has me wanting to spank her ass and pound that tight pussy. She's wound up so damn tight. "A quick fuck will do you good." I tap my fingers against the glass holding her drink. "Much better than this."

I watch her squirm in her seat under my gaze. I know I'm turning her on. She wants me just as much as I want her.

She bites her lip and swallows loudly before she says,

"At least you're being up front about it now. I knew you just wanted to fuck me." Her voice cracks at the end and betrays her confidence. I fucking love it. She's so damn innocent. I bet she's only done missionary before with some uptight, nerdy boyfriend. She's never been fucked like a woman deserves to be fucked. She tries to play off her desire by moving her book closer to the edge of the table and pretending to ignore me. That shit's not happening. I'm hard and we both need this. I shut her book and wait for her to look at me. She blurts out, "Why are you being such an asshole?" I have to stifle my grin.

"Because you keep denying yourself. Do us both a favor and stop trying to push me away." I don't understand her anger, but at least anger is something I can work with. You need passion to be angry. So I'm gonna fucking run with it. "You'll forgive me when I'm deep inside that tight pussy of yours. You need this, sweetheart, knock it the fuck off and let me take care of you."

Her breathing picks up. "I *need* this?" She huffs a humorless laugh. "What I *need* is for you to stop harassing me."

"Sweetheart, I've never seen anyone who needs a real good fuck as much as you do. Tell me you don't want me. If you can look me in the eyes and tell me to leave, I will. Cross my fucking heart." I lean forward, daring her to tell me off. I know she wants me, just like I know she needs this. I just hope she doesn't disappoint me. As she stares into my eyes searching for something, an uncomfortable feeling settles in my chest. She had better not deny me.

"Who do you think you are?" She's still playing at being offended, but I can tell she wants this. "I'm not some whore." My jaw clenches at her words. I don't like that. First a downer and then a whore. She really doesn't speak highly of herself.

"I never said that, sweetheart. I never even once had that thought. So, are you telling me to leave, or are you ready to get out of here?" Her eyes look back to her computer, breaking my gaze.

She answers with her eyes still on the screen. "I don't have my car with me." Her breathy words give me deep satisfaction. I've got my sweetheart right where I want her.

"You don't need one. We can go to the back." She gapes at me in surprise, but then her eyes widen in anger. "Relax sweetheart, this is my family's place. No one's gonna fuck with us here." Her cheeks flush pink and she turns away from me. Shit, she's embarrassed. She probably thinks I do this all the time. And I don't. I've never fucked anyone here. But I need to get inside her as soon as fucking possible. She's so damn indecisive I can't give her the chance to change her mind.

"No one's gonna know," I tell her, as I see her internally debating over what she should do. She should let me help her get this edge off. That's what she should do.

"Okay." The desperate word leaves her mouth with a primal need. She stands up and starts putting her things away, but I put my hand over hers to stop her.

"I got it, sweetheart." I put her shit in her tote as quick as I can and grip the straps in one hand. With my other hand, I take her hand in mine and pull her closer to me as I walk her to the back. I don't look around as we walk, and I'm glad she isn't looking around either. The guys may see, but they won't know for sure what I'm up to. Even if they do, they'd better not say a damn word to her. I won't let her regret this.

CHAPTER 3

ELLE

I hear a loud bang, then someone yells. The sounds are faint, and distant. What the fuck happened? I try to move my arms, but someone's holding me down. A small moan escapes from my lips. I'm so sleepy. Why am I so drowsy? I feel groggy as I turn my head slowly from side to side, and then I remember. I remember his mouth on my body. The heat between my legs makes my body want to turn and my thighs clench, but I'm pinned down. A strangled groan leaves me as I try to move my wrists, but I can't.

"She's fine." A distant, masculine voice that I don't recognize has my forehead creasing with confusion.

"If you lay another fucking hand on her, I'll--" He sounds

so angry. Why is he so angry? I struggle to remember. Vince. His handsome face and cocky smile flash before my eyes. *"I'm Vince."* I hear his words in my head. It feels like a faint memory.

"Calm down. It had to happen, Vince. This is the better alternative. For now, this should work." I hear a third voice as I start to feel slightly more alert, but I keep my eyes closed.

"I didn't fucking touch her. It's a roofie, for Christ's sake. It was either this, or off the broad." *Roofie.* That word triggers something within me, and makes me move involuntarily.

I try to jackknife off the desk, but someone's still holding me down. I open my eyes and focus on the man holding me down. I recognize his face. Vince. I struggle against him. His large frame towers over me as his dark eyes search my face. Betrayal hits me hard, and tears prick my eyes. He drugged me. Did he...? I can't even finish the thought. I struggle to breathe as a sob rips through me.

How did I get here? I'm in an office and it seems vaguely familiar. I shake my head and try to shake the sleep away. How long have I been here? I remember his face, I remember his name, I remember this room. I remember it all, but only in brief flashes. I shake my head again.

"Vince?" I ask in a wary voice. Please let me know him at least. I need to remember something.

"Shit, she remembers," one voice from over my shoulder says, and then he curses under his breath.

"She won't remember it all. I promise you this is going

to work," the third voice sounds out with confidence. Remember what?

I turn to my right to avoid looking at Vince. Fear washes over me like ice against my skin. Two large men stare back at me. Their tanned skin is stretched tight across their bulging muscles. One man is much less muscular compared to the other one, but he's still jacked. It's only because he's standing directly next to a guy with a truly beastly physique that he seems even a hair less intimidating than he actually is. Their dark hair and eyes make them a frightening sight. Mostly because they look back at me like I'm a threat. Again I try to move away, but Vince's grip only tightens on my wrists as his forearm digs deeper into my hip. My wrists burn as I continue to struggle.

Their words finally start to register and sink in. I don't know who they are or why I'm here, but I know they want to kill me. Or did. I open my mouth to scream for help out of pure instinct, but Vince is faster. He covers my mouth with his hand. I take the arm that's suddenly free and push against his hard, unmoving chest in a feeble attempt to push him away. It's useless.

Vince leans down with his lips barely touching mine. "Don't fucking do it, sweetheart." His voice holds a threat that leaves my chest hollow as fear consumes me. Who is this man? The weight of the situation crashes down on me. What the hell did I do? My eyes dart to the other men in the room.

I'm surrounded by criminals, predators who've drugged me. I close my eyes and try to will away the depressing helplessness. I'm not okay. I'm not going to be okay.

"Get out." Vince's hard voice has the two men walking slowly to the door. I concentrate on my breathing and watch them leave.

The larger of the two men looks back at Vince with a hand on the door, standing just inside the room, and holds his gaze. After a moment. Vince says softly, "I'll let you know if I need you."

Something about his tone, the somberness of it, sends pricks down my chilled skin.

The second the door shuts, I try again to get out of his grasp.

"Stop struggling." I hear the dark threat he whispers in my ear through his clenched teeth, but I don't listen. I can't listen. I saw those men. I saw the look they gave me, and then the ones they gave him. I'm fucked. I'm so fucked. They're going to kill me, and I don't even know why. I need to get the fuck out of here. I try to scream again, and the hot air and spit cover my chin as his hand presses even harder against my mouth.

"I said to stop it!" he yells. His strong arms wrap tighter around my body, and he easily lifts me up and against the wall. My heart beats frantically as I search for a way to escape. Adrenaline rushes through my blood. "Don't make me gag you." I hear his threat in my ear as tears streak down my face. I try to calm down, but all my body can do is stay tense. My muscles scream for me to move them. They want me to fight. Everything in me wants to fight. Against a man like Vince, it's hopeless.

But I can at least beg.

I stay still and try to calm my breath. My chest rises and falls with sporadic hiccups from my sobs. I need to calm the fuck down. I close my eyes and just try to breathe. He won't hurt me. I need to believe that. I need to believe there's a way out of this other than death.

As if reading my mind, he says in a calm voice, "It's going to be alright." His deep, baritone voice soothes me. It shouldn't, but it does. I shouldn't believe him. And yet, I do.

"I'm gonna take my hand away, Elle. And you're not going to scream." I attempt to nod, but his grip on me is so tight that I can't move. His hand slowly pulls back and the cool air makes it painfully obvious that I have spit all over my chin. I want to move my arms, but I'm pinned against the wall.

I turn my head slowly and see his stern expression, daring me to scream. I swallow thickly and I can't help the need to do just that. I have to try. I won't be a good little victim for him. I have to try to get the fuck out of here. My body lunges away from him without my conscious consent. The movement makes my head spin.

His large hand tightens around my throat. I struggle to breathe as my feet lift slightly off the ground. His blunt fingernails dig into the back of my neck as he shoves me against the wall. His force stuns me. But even more so, I'm shocked by the dark look in his eyes. It's a deadly look that tells me I shouldn't fuck with him. I'll regret it if I do.

I don't understand. I'm so confused. I remember glimpses of passion between us. What the fuck happened?

My hands want to reach for my throat. It's a natural instinct as my breathing comes up short. But they're pinned at my side by Vince's hip and his other hand. My eyes water, and I look back into his gaze to plead with him. I don't want to die. Not like this. Not now.

He leans into me, and the scruff on his cheek rubs against my jaw. His lips are practically touching my ear. "I don't want to hurt you, sweetheart." His breathing is unnervingly even. He's calm. Too calm. "I don't want to, but I will. I won't hesitate if you keep this shit up."

I try to stay still. With everything in me, I try to obey him, but the need to fight against his hold wins out as my vision fades and my throat seems to close.

Just as I think he's really going to end my life and choke me to death, he lets go. My feet stumble against the hard ground and I nearly roll my ankle, heaving air into my lungs. My hands feel around my throat as I land hard on my knees. I let my body sag to the ground and just breathe.

It's only then that I realize I'm crying hysterically. My face is hot and wet from the tears.

I see him bend down, his worn, dark wash jeans just an inch from me and I fall back on my butt and kick away, scrambling backward as fast as I can until I hit the wall. I restrain the scream crawling up my throat and wait as still as I can.

He's still in a squatted position, his hands resting on his knees as he looks back at me as though contemplating what to do with me. The need to fight is suppressed for now. Attempting to run would be useless. All I have left is to try and beg for mercy.

"Please let me go," I plead with him. My words are slurred. My head spins slightly as I feel the full weight of my body. I'm not okay.

"Not until I know everything you saw." His words confuse me. I don't know what he's talking about.

I shake my head violently. "I didn't see anything."

A cocky smirk graces his lips. "Sorry sweetheart, but lying isn't going to get you anywhere with me. You remembered my name."

"What did you give me?" The question comes out slower than I intend as I move my arms sluggishly and realize my motor function is off. My body heats with anxiety.

"It's a heavy sleeping pill." My head shakes. *Liar.*

"A roofie?" I ask accusingly. I remember someone saying it earlier. He drugged me. Betrayal washes through my body once again.

"It's *similar* to Rohypnol." He doesn't even have the decency to look away as he admits that they drugged me.

"Why?" I ask, in a small voice that I hope expresses my hurt.

"You saw something after we were in here, and I didn't

have much choice." His jaw clenches and he faces the wall for a moment before his gaze focuses back on me. "It was the best option at the time."

"I don't remember anything, I swear." My breath and voice both hitch in my throat. If only he'd believe me.

He sighs heavily. "It's gonna take more than that, Elle." My lips tremble and my throat dries up.

"What do I have to do?" I ask, my voice shaky.

"You need to come with me."

"Am I even going to remember this?" The thought occurs to me as I really think about what a roofie does.

"I don't know," he answers calmly. "I hope not, 'cause that would really fuck this plan up. You should still be asleep."

"I won't tell anyone." The words fly out of my mouth. I whisper hoarsely, "I swear to God, I won't." I don't care that he drugged me; I just want to get the hell out of here.

His eyes are full of remorse. "That's something we just can't risk."

"Who are you?"

He answers easily. "The mob, sweetheart." My blood chills at his confession. "You just happened to be in the wrong place at the wrong time." His eyes narrow and turn angry. "You should've waited for me." His words have a tone of accusation, but I don't even know what he's referring to.

Even with the fear from his threat still hanging over me, I manage to spit out a response in disbelief. "What did I do to deserve this?" I slam my mouth shut at the pissed off look on his face.

"That mouth, sweetheart, that mouth of yours is going to get you into trouble."

I close my eyes and pretend it's all a dream. "Please, just let me go," I whisper. After a moment, I open my eyes and find him standing, looking down at me. His broad shoulders and air of power make him the epitome of intimidation and domination. This man owns me. I am completely at his mercy.

"I'm sorry, sweetheart. I really am." He presses his lips into a straight line and shakes his head slowly. "But I'm not letting you go."

"What are you going to do with me?" My heart thuds against my chest, yet my lungs seem to freeze as I wait for his answer. He walks around the desk with his back turned to me. The sinewy muscles of his arms ripple with his movements.

He opens a drawer, and my eyes widen as I whimper and shove my body even harder into the wall. I want to look at the door. I want to search for an escape. Instead, my eyes are zeroed in on him, waiting to see what he's pulling out of the desk. I'm assuming it's a gun. I fully expect for him to shoot me.

I don't expect him to pull out thin, twined rope. It's the coarse kind that's used in kitchens. "You're going to listen to me, Elle. And I promise if you do, I'll do everything I can to keep you safe."

A mix of emotions washes over me as he pulls out more

rope and wraps it around his wrist. Surprisingly, confusion is one of the strongest ones I'm currently feeling. "Why?" I can't help asking the question. "Why are you doing this to me?"

Vince pauses his movements as his eyes find mine. His cold gaze keeps my eyes locked on his although I desperately want to look away. He responds after a long moment of silence. "Trust me, Elle. It's better this way." For the briefest second, some sick part of me does trust him. But then I quickly come to my senses.

I don't trust him. I won't.

CHAPTER 4

VINCE

What the fuck am I doing? I run my hand down my face as I hear her bang against the trunk. Again. I keep hearing her muffled screams and it's pissing me off. She doesn't listen for shit. The cold sweat that I can't kick runs through my body as I gently move the car through the intersection, past the familiar weathered stop sign. She can keep kicking and screaming for all I care. These back roads are deserted this time of day. No one is going to come save her. For now, she's mine. And that means no one's going to hurt her either.

I'll take her to the safe house in the country. It's a good 30 minutes away from here, and at least a 10 minute drive to civilization. I used to go there to hunt. Back when I thought

I'd like that shit, anyway. Turns out waking up before the crack of dawn is not my thing. So now it's the familia's. Only Dom and Pops know about it though. She'll be safe there. I run my hands through my hair and let out a heavy sigh. I'll keep her there until I know what to do about this. Until I know for sure I can save both our asses.

I wish she hadn't woken up. If she'd just stayed asleep it would've been so much better. I would've been alone, maybe told her she hit her head. I have no idea. I've never been in this situation. But I wasn't going to let them kill her. It was my fault. My fuck up. And I'm going to fix this.

The memory from earlier flashes before my eyes. Her shrill scream as she saw my cousins Anthony and Tommy hovering over the brutalized body. Blood covered nearly every inch of that poor bastard's exposed skin. My grip tightens on the steering wheel, and suddenly her relentless banging is more annoying than it was before.

I grind my teeth remembering how they came in to the office while I was trying to calm her down.

I drag her back to the room, her small body pushing against mine. Her feet barely touch the ground as I lift her squirming body to hold her tighter to my chest. Her nails dig into the skin of my forearm that's pressed hard against her chest, until I can pin her up against the back wall in the office. Her breathing is heavy and so is mine. Adrenaline courses through my blood. One hand covers her mouth to keep her screams muffled.

Fuck! I grit my teeth and keep my voice low as I speak through clenched teeth. "Stop. Screaming." She doesn't listen. She keeps it up as though I haven't said a damn thing. I slam my body up against hers, then move my hand to her throat and squeeze.

"Listen real good, you had better fucking stop." That gets her attention, but then the office door opens and two sets of heavy, even strides are heard in the silence. The door closes and locks with a loud click.

"I thought it was locked, Vince." Anthony speaks, but I don't turn around. I keep my eyes on hers as they dart to my cousins behind me.

"You want me to do it quick, Vince?" Anthony asks. "I'll make it painless."

My blood chills as I watch her eyes widen in fear. My poor sweetheart. I can't. I can't let that happen.

"No." It's the only word I can say. I don't want to explain it to them. Because I'm their boss, I should know what to do, but I haven't got a clue.

"You need her to talk or something, Vince?" I can hear the confusion in Anthony's voice. She should be dead by now. I shouldn't be toying with her like this. Thing is though, I don't want her dead. She whimpers and her eyes finally meet mine. I know I must look like a cold-blooded killer. My jaw is clenched and my eyes are hard.

She struggles again in my grasp and then I remember my forearm on her neck. Her head is pushed back in an unnatural way and she's taking in ragged breaths. I let up on my grip.

I place my lips at her ear and whisper, "Don't you make a fucking sound."

"Vince?" At Anthony's question, I turn my shoulder to Elle. And she acts like a fucking idiot and takes off behind me. My hand reaches out to snatch her but I miss. Tommy's right fucking there, though. Did she really think she'd make it? Watching Tommy wrap an arm around her waist, bringing her body up against his pisses me off.

He speaks clearly, and I can hear the remorse in his voice as he says, "I'm sorry, I really am."

I know exactly what he's gonna do. He's planning on snapping her neck. Quick, painless, but it's not going to fucking happen. I take three strides and I'm on him. I land my fist on his jaw like a fucking asshole. He doesn't see it coming, and it sends him flying into the wall. His shoulder blade hits the drywall, leaving a large dent. Elle tumbles to the ground and I step over her, fuming with rage.

"No one touches her. No one!" I scream so loud I know they all hear it. Everyone in this place. But I don't give a fuck. It's not going down like this. I know the rules, just like I know I'm breaking them right now. But I don't care. I'm not going to allow anyone to hurt her.

I hear her shriek, and I turn to see Anthony holding her just like Tommy was. But he's quick to respond. "Just keeping her from running, boss." I give him a quick nod and turn back to Tommy. He's looking up at me with equal amounts of shock and aggression.

I reach down and offer my hand and help him up. His eyes stay on me, waiting.

"I don't want her dead, Tommy." He looks at me for a moment and then nods.

"One second, boss." I don't know what he has planned. But I do know this is all fucked.

It's all my fault. All of it.

What the hell was I doing letting her leave on her own? Fucking careless. I was sloppy. I'm not fucking sloppy. Never. That's not how Valettis do business. I grind my teeth and look out of the window as we finally leave the outskirts of the city. Pops is going to be pissed.

Just the thought of his disappointment makes my heart sink. I don't really give too much of a shit what anyone thinks of me, except for Pops and Ma. Sometimes my brother Dom and sister Clara. But my father's opinion matters the most. He's always been proud of me. But this shit I've gotten us into--this is not good. He's not going to fucking like that I risked the family to get my dick wet at our place of business.

I don't know what it is about this broad that has me making poor decisions left and right. I don't know if it's her curves, that little pout she has that shows me she's hurting, or that snappy little attitude that comes out of nowhere.

I fucking love the spitfire my sweetheart is. I can't fucking wait for her to go off on me again so I can spank that ass of hers. Next thing I know my dick's hard, pressing against my zipper. I let my head fall back, but keep my eyes on the road. And then I hear her thumping away in the back. What the fuck is wrong with me? I'm never getting in that pussy again. I'm the fucking enemy now.

She probably doesn't even remember that hot as fuck pregaming session we had. Shit. She'd better not. She'd better not remember anything more than my name. I shift uncomfortably in my seat and let out a deep sigh. This is so fucked.

At that thought I realize I have no fucking clue what I'm gonna do with her now. I could bring her to my room and pretend we had a one-night stand. That makes sense. I took her out to the bar, we got drunk, had a great night together. Boom, it's done and over with. My chest pains at the thought. I don't want it to be over with. I don't like that option. But I'm sure as shit not bringing her around the family after this. Tommy and Anthony are the only ones that know. They know better than to tell Pops. That's my job. My responsibility.

I look down at the watch and see it's been two hours since she woke up. That means she's gonna need another dose soon. She shouldn't remember any of this shit with that drug in her system.

Calling it a sleeping aid was a shit thing to do. It wasn't a blatant lie, but it's not like I'm gonna tell her I roofied her. I don't want to give her the impression that we do that kind of shit on vulnerable women, 'cause we don't. It comes in handy when you wanna take out someone high up though. It's much easier to take a knocked out fucker to the pits than having to fight him on his own territory. Of course she didn't get the same dose we use for that kind of thing. It's hard to know how much even got into her system though. Tommy just shoved it in her mouth, and as a result she nearly bit his finger off.

My stomach knots and twists. I'm kidnapping and drugging this woman. What a fucking low point in my life. I really hope this fucking works. Anthony swore by it. He's real fucking good at getting information from people, and when he asks what happened right before he drugged them and they still don't know even after spending an hour on his table, then they really have no fucking clue. And that means the drug works. It had better work. But she remembered my name. Tomorrow morning, I need to determine everything she remembers.

I put my hand on the seat of my Audi just like normal, and that's when I realize Rigs isn't with me.

Fuck. I look into the rear-view mirror and there's no one

there. I can't risk going back to my place with her in the trunk though. I'll have to go back later to pick up my dog. I'll drop her off at the safe house, and then I'll go back to my place in the city to pick up his furry little ass. I sure as hell can't leave him at my place by himself. He'd probably chew up the coffee table just to spite me. I really hope he didn't shit in my house though. I swear puppies are worse than babies. They have to be. Dom's little one just chews on the toys they give him and he can't move, like a little sack of potatoes.

A small grin kicks my lips up, but it vanishes when I hear another bang from the trunk. Fucking hell. I wish she'd calm her ass down. She's gonna think we had some real rough sex last night and that I tied her ass up. I groan and adjust my cock as it twitches with need. I'd love to fuck this woman. I want inside her more than I've ever wanted anything before. But there's no way that's happening, not with all this shit.

I really fucked this up.

CHAPTER 5

ELLE

My wrists burn as the rope chafes against them. But I don't stop struggling. I won't stop. I know if I can just get my hands free then I'll be able to untie my legs. There's enough room for me to wiggle around and search for the latch. There's always a latch in these cars.

I take a deep, extremely unsteady breath and focus on loosening the knot. My shoulders hurt so fucking bad. Every bump we go over sends my body bouncing and I land hard on my side. I have nothing to brace my head against either. My neck hurts from trying to brace myself every time we hit a bump.

My throat is killing me from screaming and my eyes feel raw. It's a horrible feeling, knowing you're going to die. I just don't understand why he hasn't done it yet. He's not going to let me go. More tears prick at my eyes. My hand covers my mouth to hold back the sob. He's keeping me. My body shivers and I pull my legs up to my chest and rock myself.

I can't believe this is what I am now. A prisoner. He's going to do whatever he wants with me. I'm completely at his mercy. The tears fall down my face. I rub my cheek on my knee, to wipe the tears away, and try to steady my breath. Maybe that's not it. Or maybe I can appeal to that side of him. A flicker of hope lights inside of me. I just need to get out of here. However I can.

I'm so god damn tired. I feel dizzy and my head is killing me. I just want to go to sleep, but I can't. I want to fight this. I don't want to fall asleep. I can't just lie down and let him do whatever the fuck he wants with me. I'm going to fight as long as I can. Confusion overwhelms me again. I just don't understand why my memory is so passionate, giving me a feeling of comfort and safety, but my reality is the exact opposite.

The brakes slow again, and this time the car stills and I hear the click of him parking the car. My heartbeat picks up to a frantic pace. I failed. I couldn't get out of these fucking ropes or find a trunk latch anywhere. Fear cripples me as he pops open the trunk. I try to scream through the gag, but it's useless.

"Come on sweetheart, did you really think I'd take you to somewhere you would be heard?" He looks at me like he's disappointed. I don't know what he expects from me. "Be a good girl for me and make things easy for us both, alright?" Is he out of his god damned mind?

I try to scoot away from him, but it's useless. It's not like there's a ton of extra room in the trunk. I don't even realize he's untying the rope around my legs though until he starts massaging my calves. A moan of satisfaction leaves me. I didn't realize how sore they were until he brought more circulation to them. His large, rough hands move to my wrists and as the ease of comfort coupled with slight pain hits me, he rubs my shoulders, bringing them back to life.

"I'm sorry about that," he apologizes, and he sounds truly sincere. His thumbs move in small circles on my back, and then travel up to my shoulders and down my arms. "But you weren't really cooperating."

His excuse pisses me off. What he's doing is not fucking okay. I can't remember a damn thing. Ergo, there's no reason for me to be here. They should've just let me go. I close my eyes as his soothing touch relieves the ache. I try to remember.

I recall that moment when he introduced himself with his handsome smirk after I heard his deep masculine voice state, *"I'm Vince."* That moment flashes before me and sends a warmth through my body. That memory is followed by the feeling of my back arching on the hard, cold desk while his mouth licks and sucks at my clit. Fuck! I force my heavy eyes open as his arms wrap around me, bringing me close to his hot, hard body. I push away from him and snap, "I can walk."

His pissed off expression makes me want to cower, but he slowly puts me down and lets my feet find purchase on the ground.

I hate that I gave myself to him. I clench my thighs again. I don't feel any different. I'm not sore at all. More than anything, my clit is swollen with the need for his touch. I have no idea what all we did, but it's more than I've ever done before, at least on the receiving end. I've never had anyone go down on me. My cheeks flame with embarrassment.

I take one step forward with his hand resting lightly on the small of my back. I look up at the house. It's not large, but it's not small either. A country home, with light blue shutters and a porch swing. It looks like a picture-perfect home, out in the middle of nowhere with a dirt driveway. My eyes dart to the left--nothing but a flat field. My eyes dart to the right--woods.

Seeing the woods and knowing we're alone terrifies me. My body turns to ice.

He's going to kill me. My feet stumble and I nearly lose my balance. I take a ragged breath. I can't do this. Anxiety makes my blood race and adrenaline pumps through my veins. I can't handle this shit. My throat closes.

"You okay?" Vince asks me, and again I'm confused by the concern in his voice. I don't know what's going on. I wish I could remember. I swallow thickly and nod my head, righting myself. I wish all this were over with. I close my eyes and remember how he choked me against the wall. I can't. I can't go in there with him. I won't make it out alive.

I may not be strong, but I don't have to be. Not physically, anyway. I push my heavy body forward and shove my elbow right into his spleen. I saw someone do it in a movie once. I hear a gush of air push out of him and his groan of pain as he topples forward, but I don't waste a second. I force my body to move and sprint toward the woods. Everything is a blur. My heart isn't steady, and my ankle nearly rolls, but I push forward. I lose one of my flats, but I don't spare a moment to even consider it.

My bare foot pounds against the grass as I race to the edge of the woods. I can hear him getting up. He'll catch up to me in no time. If only I can get into the woods far enough to hide. It's dark out. I can hide. I need to be able to hide. My feet slam against the ground. I feel the cold dirt on the sole of my bare foot. My heart hammers faster. Branches whip by my face. I duck to avoid as many as I can. I brace my body against a thick tree trunk and try to keep my balance. The rough bark scratches against my skin.

I heave in a breath and then scream as Vince's body slams into mine, knocking me to the ground. His large body pins me down. His hips spread my legs apart and his knees land on my thighs, pushing my body open and forcing me to stay beneath him. He pins my wrists above my head with one hand, and his other hand wraps around my throat. I let out a scream, but he doesn't put any pressure on my throat.

Instead, he's just merely gripping it. I try to buck him off of me, but it's hopeless.

He growls into my ear. "You can't fucking listen, can you?" I close my eyes and whimper.

"I don't want to die." My murmur is barely more than a whisper.

"You're not fucking acting like it." His hand tightens on my throat, and his hips push harder into mine.

For a moment my eyes flash to an image of him on top of me, pounding into me, ruthlessly rutting between my legs. My body heats at the thought. I can see us just like this. I turn my head to the side and refuse to think about it. My body flames with need, but I deny it. I'm so ashamed. So confused.

"You need to fucking listen to me." He clenches his teeth and slowly lets go of my wrists. I don't move. I stay as still as possible. He grips my chin and forces me to look at him, but I keep my eyes closed. He squeezes tighter and I instinctively open my eyes. His sharp, dark gaze stares back at me.

"Don't fight me," he commands. "You will obey me." His words send another shot of arousal through me, but thankfully he's already on his feet and pulling my nearly limp body up onto his. He slings me over his shoulder to carry me away like some kind of primitive caveman.

I don't know what to think. I don't understand why I feel this way.

I don't have a choice in any of this.

CHAPTER 6

VINCE

I can't believe she fucking ran. My blunt fingernails dig into a tender part of her waist as I drag her body back to the house, with my hand gripping her hip. She's not walking fast enough, not making this easy, but at least she's not fighting.

"That wasn't a smart thing for you to do, sweetheart," I mumble under my breath. I'm pissed off. I'm really fucking pissed off. I'm trying to help this girl. I'm going out of my way and risking my own ass for hers. If she got out... My blood runs cold thinking what would happen. For a split second, the choice is obvious. I can't allow it to happen. There's only one way to make sure she never talks. I don't trust that she got a high enough dose. And neither will the *familia*.

I shake my head and pull her closer to me. "Walk with

me, Elle. Stop making this so fucking hard." My voice reflects my anger. She quickens her pace and I take a look at her as we near the porch. Her face is red from panting, her cheeks stained with tears. Her shirt's ripped from falling down earlier, and there are scrapes on her knees.

My heart sinks in my chest. I'm such a fucking asshole for being angry with her. I'd run, if I were in her shoes. First chance I got, I'd fucking bolt. How can I blame her? She has no idea what's going on. Other than the fact that I'm not letting her go, and that some people in the *familia* want her dead.

I look down at her feet. She lost one shoe somewhere back there, and her bare foot is dirty and bleeding from running through the forest. My poor sweetheart. I stop at the door and sigh. "Are you going to listen to me?"

Her wide, frightened eyes dart to mine. She slowly nods her head. She's fucking lying. I can see it written on her face. "Don't make me chase after you again, sweetheart." I move my hand up to the nape of her neck and fist her hair. I pull slightly, which gets me a small whimper, and lean down to let my lips barely touch her ear. "Next time I won't be nearly as nice." I whisper my threat and let my hot breath send a shiver down her body. I let go of her and open the door with my back to her, giving her the chance to fucking defy me. Again.

The sound of her heavy, shaky exhale make my chest hurt. I feel like such a fucking asshole. But what the hell am I supposed to do? It'll be better tomorrow. As long as she doesn't remember what she witnessed earlier at the bistro, everything will be better. If she remembers though, I'm fucked. She can't remember any of this shit. And that reminds me about the tablets in my pocket.

I unlock the door and walk in, holding the door open for her. She sways slightly on her feet and looks behind her. A low growl vibrates through my chest, making her head snap back around as she looks at me with wide eyes.

"Come on in, sweetheart." I can't help my narrowed eyes and threatening stare, but at least my voice isn't completely menacing. She swallows loudly and slowly walks in. I can see she's tired. She's fighting this shit, even though it should've knocked her on her ass. That makes me worry even more. She walks in slowly and at an angle. She keeps her eyes on me but keeps her distance, staying more than an arm's reach away.

I shut the door and lock it. The loud click of the lock makes her eyes dart to the doorknob. I practically see her heart beating out of her chest as her breathing picks up. I can tell she's on the verge of a panic attack. If only she'd just sleep. Just go to bed and make this easy on both of us.

My heart twists with agony as I watch her eyes dart around the foyer like something's going to come out of a dark corner and attack her. I need to help put her at ease. As much as I can, anyway.

"Are you hungry?" I've got this place stocked with food, no fresh stuff though. I'll pick some up when I get Rigs. I clench my jaw. I'm gonna have to tie her up to do that. She's not going to like it. But there's no fucking way I'm risking anything at this point.

She's quick to shake her head no.

"Did you eat before you went out tonight?" I ask calmly. She tilts her head to one side as though she's thinking. "Do you remember?" I prompt.

"I'm not hungry." Her voice is small, but even.

"That's not what I asked." I manage to keep most of the irritation out of my statement.

"Yes I remember, and no I didn't eat," she responds quickly.

I nod and take a step towards her, but she takes a step back. She's cornering herself in, but she has nowhere to go anyway. She won't be getting away from me now.

"I want you to eat something, and then I have to leave for a bit." I watch as her eyes light up at the thought of being alone. It pisses me off. All of this pisses me off. If she hadn't been so damn eager to leave earlier at the bistro, I could've had her cumming on my dick right now. Instead she's scared of me, when I'm the one busting ass to keep her alive.

"Stop running from me," I practically snarl. I take in a deep breath through my nose as my anger rises. I reach out and grab her waist before she can back away, pulling her small body to mine. Her hips press against mine. "Let's get one thing straight, Elle." I wrap my hand along her upper neck and use my thumb to push up her chin so that she's forced to look me in the eyes. "You fucking wanted me, before all this shit happened. You wanted me, and then you left me. You got yourself into this shit, and now I'm saving your ass."

Her eyes widen as though she's surprised. And I'm not sure which part triggered that response. I lower my lips closer to hers. "The least you can do is make this easy on me."

Her light blue eyes stare into mine. She parts her lips and all I want to do is take them with my own. I want to make this easy. I want to make it right. But when she speaks, it ends that desire.

"I don't trust you." The softly whispered words hit my chest like fucking bullets.

It fucking hurts, but I can't say that I'm too surprised. It takes a lot for me to trust a person, too. "Fair enough. Maybe you can make it easier on yourself then and stop pissing off your captor." My stomach drops as I refer to myself that way. But that's exactly who I am to her. Not her fucking savior, that's for damn sure. I'm the enemy.

"Does that sound like a smart thing to do, Elle?" I ask her as I tilt my head.

"No." Her plump lips stay parted as she answers me, and her eyes fall to my throat. A sadness washes over her. Her eyes stay on the dip of my throat as she asks, "What are you going to do to me?" I can hear the obvious defeat in her tone. I suppose in a way that's good, but it crushes me. I don't want to kill the bit of spitfire she has.

"I'm going to feed you." I tilt up her chin again to make

sure she gives me her full attention. I repeat, "I'm going to feed you, but then I have to tie you up again so I can leave." She takes a quick inhale and her nostrils flare, but she keeps her mouth shut before nodding at me.

I pull back and walk away from her towards the kitchen. I turn to look over my shoulder. "Come." Her feet move obediently at the command.

"When you wake up tomorrow, this will all be over. Everything will be perfect," I say, trying to sound reassuring. I listen to her feet moving slowly behind me as I enter the modern kitchen. I turn to look at her as I reach the pantry. "You won't remember anything, and everything will be just as it was." I fill a glass with water and set it on the counter. I debate against showing her what I'm about to do, but ultimately I decide to show her. I don't want to trick her.

I reach in my pocket and pull out the bottle with the tablets. I pop the top off and drop one of the tablets into the glass.

I pick up the glass and watch as the tablet quickly dissolves into nothing. Her full, plump lips frown as I take a step toward her. "Drink this, sweetheart." I hold out the glass and her small hands reach out to accept it from me. Her fingers overlap as she lifts the glass to her lips. I'll have a good hour to hour and a half with her before she should pass out with this dose.

She stares at the glass for a moment and I consider pushing her, but I don't. Thankfully she puts it to her lips and downs the water completely. With the glass empty, she gently places it on the counter, with her eyes on the floor and drenched in defeat.

Her mouth opens as her fingers toy with the loops on her shorts. But she slams it shut and instead focuses her gaze on the slate tiles on the kitchen floor. She looks so beaten down. She looks hopeless. She's covered in dirt and scratches. I'm going to need to bathe her. She can't wake up like that.

Her eyes reach mine with sadness and her mouth opens and then closes again. "What is it?" I ask, with patience and comfort.

"Please don't touch me." Her shoulders rise and her body trembles as she swallows thickly and moves her gaze back to the floor. She clasps her hands in front of her. My forehead creases with confusion, and then I realize the meaning of her words. I close my eyes and give myself a moment.

When I open them, her hands are covering her face as she stands there in the middle of my kitchen. She doesn't belong here. It's so fucking obvious to me that this is fucked up.

"Elle, sweetheart..." I walk over to her and wrap my arms around her so that she can lay her head against my chest. She's stiff at first, but I rub up and down her back with comforting strokes. "I would never do that to you." I kiss her hair and continue rubbing soothing circles on her back.

"I promise you. I won't hurt you."

CHAPTER 7

ELLE

"I'm not leaving you alone again, and I've already seen you naked, so just strip." I stand with my back to Vince as I face the shower. I can't believe he's serious. I can't believe any of this. He tried to get me to eat, but I'm so sick to my stomach. And now he wants to bathe me. I can't wash myself, thank you very much.

"I can--" I start to say the words in the softest, most respectful tone I can manage, but he cuts me off.

"I'm not leaving you for one second." I turn around slowly. His muscular arms are crossed, pulling his tee shirt tighter over his chest. It makes the muscles in his shoulders and arms bulge.

I look up at him through my thick lashes. "I promise--"

"I'm staying right here." His words are absolute. "You're going to be tired soon. You could pass out in the stall. I'm not leaving."

I take in a deep breath and close my eyes, and pull my tank top over my head and unhook my bra, removing them both quickly before I hurriedly shove my shorts down. I step out of them and quickly walk underneath the hot cascade of water. I wince as the heat bites into the small scrapes on my body. They aren't that bad. Tomorrow they'll start to scab over and not look like much of anything. I open my mouth and let the water hit my face.

Tomorrow I won't remember. I hope I don't.

I feel like a coward for thinking that. But I really don't want to remember this. I've given up. If I do remember, I'm going to pretend like hell that I don't remember.

"Here." I jump at the sound of Vince's voice and nervously watch as he hands me bottles of cheap shampoo and conditioner. They're small bottles like you'd expect to find in a hotel bathroom. I reach out and take them both with one hand. I have to close my eyes as our fingers touch. I feel so alone. That must be why I want him. It's the only reason I can think of as to why I'm feeling this way.

I don't know which emotion is stronger. The fear that he's going to kill me, or the desire for him to fuck me. My conscience is raging war within me. One moment I want him to use me. Yet the next moment, I'm afraid he's going to touch me. It's as though my fantasies and nightmares have combined into a reality. And I'm not sure which is which anymore.

I open my eyes and I find him staring at me. He looks like a caged beast. His hands grip the edge of the stall and he leans in just slightly. "Do you need anything else?" he asks. I know exactly what he's asking, and the answer is no. I quickly shake my head no and open the first bottle. The other I set down on a shelf. He pushes off the wall and steps backward, but I can feel his eyes on me.

I clean off as quickly as I can. I've already submitted. I can only hope tomorrow I'll forget. Tomorrow I'll wake up, and he'll take me back home. Then all of this won't even be a nightmare.

It simply won't exist.

I close my eyes again and feel a fog set in. I welcome it.

I lean my back against the cold tile wall and vaguely hear Vince's voice speaking. But it fades in the distance, and suddenly his face is in front of me with that handsome smirk. *"I'm Vince."* I hear his confident, masculine voice. I see him lift his head away from my heat and stare up at my body as a wave of heat rolls through me. Another flash, a mix of memories. And then my body seems to go weightless.

Darkness sets in.

The last thing I hear before I pass out gives me a sense of peace and calm that I'm not sure I've ever felt. "I've got you, sweetheart."

CHAPTER 8

VINCE

I park in front of my house and sit in the car to take a quick mental inventory of everything before I go in there. It took a good bit to get over here, but I still haven't had enough time to process all this shit. Pops' car is out front. I know he's waiting for me inside. I sent him a text letting him know I had something I needed to talk to him about, and I know he's gonna be sweating his balls off with worry. I grip the wheel with both hands, remembering how I left her at the safe house.

She's only in an old Henley shirt of mine. Both wrists are tied to the bed frame. I think she's comfortable. I hope she is. I hate leaving her like that, but I have to get my dog. I already picked up some food for breakfast, and some clothes for her to wear. But right now I have to talk to Pops. The Don. I tap the wheel a few times and finally get the fuck out of the car. I might as well get this over with.

He's standing in the living room, and I see him as soon as I walk in. His eyes are on me as I toss the keys on the table and bend down to greet Rigs. My black lab is all muscle, with a long-ass tail that thumps onto walls as he wags it. He licks my face and I try to smile. But I can't.

"You alright, son?" My father's words wipe my pathetic attempt to smile right off my face. A thick feeling of sickness settles in my stomach.

I stand up and head to the living room. "I think everything's going to be alright. I just have something to tell you."

His facial expression doesn't change when he hears this. There's a hint of worry in his eyes, but other than that, nothing.

"What's going on, Vince?" His voice is hard, like it always is. Pops is old now, with grey in his hair, and wrinkles around his eyes. But he's still got a hard edge. Anyone who's ever met him wouldn't find it hard to believe he's the boss, 'cause he looks like and acts like the boss. I've always looked up to him. But right now, I'm finding it hard to look him in the eyes.

"It's basically taken care of, but I fucked up." I take a seat on the sofa, and Rigs hops up next to me and tries to sit in my lap. He's 6 months old or so now, not exactly the little puppy he was when I first got him. But, I really don't mind it. He can still keep thinking he's a tiny lapdog when he's 80 pounds for all I care. I give Rigs a few pats, then look my father square in the eyes.

"I fucked up and because of me a broad walked in on Tommy and Anthony." There, it's out. My father's expression stays flat.

"I see. That's very disappointing." His jaw is clenched tight and he keeps his eyes on me as he takes a seat to my left. "And it's *basically* taken care of?" He cocks an eyebrow at me.

"I couldn't let them fix it the way we normally take care of that." Witnesses don't exist to us, because if they see anything that could threaten the *familia*, they're dead. That's just how it works.

"What do you mean?" His eyes narrow. "What all did she see?"

"She walked in at the end of an interrogation."

"And where is she now?" Although his words are calm, I can practically hear his heart racing and waves of anger rolling off of him.

"At the safe house. The cabin." The look of sheer disappointment from my father crushes me. He leans forward with his head resting in his hands and his elbows on his knees. "Pops, she's not going to remember. Tommy gave her some of the roofies we use."

Pops looks pissed.

"What was I supposed to do? Kill her? It was my fault, I know, but I'm taking care of it." My voice raises in anger, and I almost regret it. Almost.

"Are you fucking kidding me?" he asks with disdain.

I press my lips into a tight line and shake my head. "What were you doing, Vince? What was so important to you that you let a broad back there to see that?"

"I said I fucked up." I'm getting more and more pissed off listening to him tear me a new one. Yeah, I know what I did was wrong. I shouldn't have taken her back there, back at the bistro. I fucking forgot what was going on.

"And if she remembers? When she wakes up, if she remembers, are you going to kill her?" I look over his face and I have no clue what he wants me to say. My gut roils and I know I wouldn't want to kill her. But what choice will I have?

"All this, just to get your dick wet, Vince?" He asks sarcastically. God damn, does he have to twist the knife?

"Pops, you don't understand."

"Explain it to me then. I'd love to know what was going on in that head of yours that you failed to do the one thing you were in charge of."

I lay my head back against the sofa and stare at the ceiling. I run a hand over my face in exasperation. "I can't tell you. I just felt like--" He cuts me off.

"Like what? Horny? Is that it?" He's still pissed and I get it, I really do. I'm pissed, too. But give me a fucking break. I didn't let it get out of hand. I'm fixing this shit.

I open my eyes and stare back at my father with daggers in my eyes. "It was more than that."

His brows raise in disbelief. "Oh? Is that right?" He looks at me expectantly and still I don't know what to tell him.

"I told you, I fucked up. But I'm taking care of it. Tomorrow she'll be gone."

My father stares back at me with a look of contemplation. I wish he'd just give the okay. That's what I need from him, but instead he pushes me further. "How are you going to know for sure that she doesn't remember?"

I don't. That's the fucked up part. If she's a really good actress, I could be fucked. But I'm not going to tell him that. I can't. I don't want her dead. But I know I shouldn't be taking risks like this.

Pops looks at me like he can read my mind. "Bring her to dinner tomorrow."

"Pops, I don't want to hurt her."

"Sounds like you already did, Vince." He stands up and waits for me. I have to move Rigs to get up, and he doesn't like it, vocalizing his displeasure with a soft whine.

"I feel like shit."

He smirks at me. "That's exactly how you look, too."

I roll my eyes, but he's probably telling the truth. "I'm going to make this right."

He nods his head and then looks out the window. "I hope she forgets, Vince. I really do." He gives me a quick hug, coupled with a stern pat on the back. His hand goes to my shoulder and he squeezes. "If it means anything to you,

I think you made the right decision." He releases me and breathes in deep. "It's not her fault." His eyes find mine again. "Let me know before dinner if she's coming." He purses his lips thoughtfully, but then he frowns. "If not, and you need help, you can call me if you need."

My blood chills. I know that's the only other option. But I fucking hate it.

I finally answer, "She'll be at dinner." He nods his head with a grim smile as he walks me to the door.

He watches me leave, and it's not until my house is out of sight that the true weight of the situation settles heavily against my chest.

I'll go back and untie her ass, but I'm staying close. I just have to wait until she wakes up. Then I'll know what I have to do.

If she remembers, I'm going to have to kill her. I don't have a fucking choice.

CHAPTER 9

ELLE

Oh. My. God. My head is fucking killing me. I roll over onto my side and throw my hand out to my nightstand for my water. Every night I put my glass in the same spot, right after taking melatonin to help me get some rest. When my hand falls onto nothing, my heavy eyelids open slowly. I jackknife off the bed. Oh shit, I forgot I'm at Mom's. I rub my eyes and then look around. This is not Mom's.

My heart races in my chest. I look down at myself and see small marks on my wrists that burn slightly to the touch. There are a few small scrapes on my knees. Most importantly, I'm wearing a very large grey Henley shirt that's not mine. What the fuck did I do last night?

My eyes dart across the bedroom. Judging from the décor,

I'd guess that this is a man's bedroom. The walls are a dark grey. The comforter is a slightly lighter shade of grey, while the bed sheets are white. The furniture is modern; a mix of clean lines and dark, stained wood. There isn't a single thing out of place. Nothing that really denotes any personality, either. No picture frames, nothing. There's a gun safe in the corner. It's taller than me.

Where the fuck am I? I pull my knees to my chest as I scan around the room some more, searching for my purse or clothes. I don't see anything. My gut churns with nausea. What the fuck happened last night?

I close my eyes and try to remember. Ugh. Mother. I'm so fucking pissed at my mother. The very thought makes my head hurt. My temples throb with pain. I remember being pissed off and leaving, but that's it. I wanted to study.

That's a fucking lie.

I wanted to get away. Just like I always do. Run and hide away in my books.

Shit! Thinking about work and studying reminds me that I have to study those chapters for my presentation in class. Where the hell is my stuff? I remember leaving, but I can't think of anything else.

The sound of the door opening startles me. I watch as the most gorgeous man I've ever laid eyes on walks in with a silver tray in his hands. His eyes stay on the cups on the tray while he kicks a foot behind him to shut the door. He takes a few steps toward the bed and my mouth falls open as I stare at him.

He's a fucking sex god. He's wearing blue plaid pajama pants that are slung low on his hips, revealing how cut his body is. That sexy "V" at the hips that I've only ever seen before on porn stars or male underwear models is on full display, and right smack in the middle is a thin happy trail of hair. His broad chest is very impressive, but it's his shoulders that get me. Holy fuck. I have a thing for shoulders. His dark eyes meet mine, and he grins at me.

"I'm surprised you're not drooling, sweetheart." His deep, masculine voice makes my clit throb with need, but more than that, it triggers a memory. A cocky smirk, then his handsome smile. *"I'm Vince."* I hear his voice in my head.

"Vince?" I feel awkward asking, but I really don't remember a thing.

His smile falters for a moment and it makes me feel guilty for forgetting whatever happened. Oh. God. What did happen? I clench my thighs and I don't feel any different. I feel horny as hell. But not... sore. Another memory flashes in front of my eyes. Oh fuck. He totally ate me out. My cheeks flame with embarrassment.

"You alright, sweetheart?" He sets the tray down on the nightstand. "You're acting a little off."

I swallow hard and look at him, and then down at the tray. Aw. He made pancakes and cut up some fruit. There's orange juice, plus the distinct smell of coffee. Thank fuck! My head is killing me. I could really use the caffeine. I hesitate to tell him I don't remember last night. Instead I crawl on the bed toward him and quickly grab a cup of coffee. I make sure my ass stays under the covers, though. For all I know it's just my hormones that are making me so horny over this guy, and he doesn't want me like that. Although the way his eyes follow my body as I move, suggests that he does.

I sit back and get settled. I have to tell him. I feel awful for practically forgetting his name. Obviously *something* happened between us. And that flicker of memory warms my chest, so it must be something good.

"I have a really bad headache right now."

His eyes look over my face. "You want an aspirin?" When I shake my head gently and blow on the coffee, he sits down on the bed. "I brought up sugar and creamer too if you'd like."

I smile into the steam rising off the cup and take a small sip. Damn, that's good coffee. "No thanks, I like it black."

He grins at me. "Low-maintenance, I see."

A nervous laugh leaves my lips. It's quiet for a moment while he grabs his cup.

"Hey Vince?" I ask. My questioning tone has his eyebrows raising in response.

"Yeah, Elle?" He sets his coffee down without taking a sip. "What's up, sweetheart?"

God I feel like an asshole. He's so sweet with the breakfast and the nickname. I just blurt it out. "I kinda think maybe I drank too much last night?" I've never been blackout drunk before, but my friend from undergrad Viv drank till she was shitfaced all the time. It scares me that I was so reckless last night. I was so pissed off. I should be smarter than that. But at least I'm still alive and I didn't get into any trouble. I clench my thighs again. At least I don't feel like I did, anyway.

He let out a sexy chuckle that shakes the bed. It makes me smile, then he smirks back at me. "Yeah, you were keeping up with me, and I drink a lot." He lies across the bed, propping himself up with his elbow. "At least tell me you remember something specific about last night."

I blush and suck down the rest of the coffee in a rush. "I mean, of course I remember *some* things." I nervously set the coffee mug down on the tray again.

"Tell me baby, I wanna know what I did that was so memorable." Oh my god, I'm practically swooning from his charm. His handsome smile makes me blush even more. I bite my lip and shake my head.

"You *know* what I remember," I say as I roll my eyes at him playfully. I see the marks on my wrists again, and then my throat seems to go dry. I don't remember how those marks got there. "How did I get hurt?"

His eyes travel to my wrists and then he looks back up at my face. "Not sure, sweetheart. I didn't notice them until just now." That makes me feel a bit uneasy. I wish I could remember.

"Did we...?" *Have sex.* I can't even say it out loud. God, I'm such a child. I don't know why I avoid this shit. Thank fuck I've been on birth control since I was 16 for acne. I try to remember if I took my pill yesterday morning, and I'm sure I did. I bite my bottom lip, knowing I need to take today's pill sometime soon.

"Did we what, sweetheart?" He grins at me. "I wanna hear you say it."

I roll my eyes again and pretend to blow him off. But my heart twists in my chest. Did I really have sex last night? And I don't even remember?

"We didn't," he says after a few seconds. Relief floods through me.

"So we didn't have sex?" I ask, just to clarify. I clench my legs again and I'm certain I don't feel any different. Horny as all hell, but not like I got myself fucked for the first time last night.

He pouts and it makes me wanna kiss his plump lips. "We did fool around though. I happen to enjoy that mouth of yours." That sexy smirk is back and if I wasn't so shy, I'd crawl forward and nip his bottom lip. In my head it'd be sexy, but in reality... Nope, not going to make a fool of myself in the first five minutes of talking with this guy.

A violent blush rushes to my cheeks. I look around the room again. I don't see my clothes or my bag.

"Do you know where I left my stuff?" I change the subject to avoid thinking about sex some more.

"Uh, yeah. Your laptop is downstairs, and since I ruined your clothes I went out and got you some new ones." On his last word the door pops open, and a dog comes barreling into the room.

"Rigs, down!" Vince yells in a commanding tone, but the dog hops on the bed anyway and runs straight toward me.

I let out a squeal as the puppy rushes forward and puts both of his large heavy front paws on me. He's not quite a fully grown adult dog yet, but he's gotta be getting close, judging from his size. It's hard to hold him back as I laugh and he slobbers all over my mouth. I have to keep my lips pressed tightly shut so he doesn't accidentally French kiss me.

"That's it, Rigs!" I hear Vince's voice boom over my laughs, and suddenly the dog is gone. I watch him put Rigs outside the door and close it.

My cheeks hurt from smiling so hard. And as he turns and gives me the sexiest grin I've ever seen, I feel a blush rise up my chest and into my cheeks.

I don't remember last night, but this morning is looking like it's going to be good.

CHAPTER 10

VINCE

God damn, she's so cute. There's not a doubt in my mind that she's forgotten everything. The only scars from yesterday are the small marks on her body. And fuck me, but I want to put more on her. Her sexy laugh and her rolling her eyes at me make me want to jump into bed and fuck her. I never had the chance before. I debate on getting into bed. I know I'm gonna have to leave this broad. I can't bring her around everyone. It's best if she just stays away.

But she did want me yesterday. And now that all this shit is done with, maybe it's not so wrong.

She crawls toward me like a cat, and it makes her ass peek out slightly from the hem of my shirt. That's the final straw. She wants me, and I want her. Nothing else matters right now. I lift her hips up with both hands and toss her onto her back. She lets out a sexy squeal that makes Rigs bark and paw at the door. But he's gonna have to stay outside for this.

She laughs again, but then seems to remember that she doesn't remember last night fully, and her shyness comes back to her. She tries to right herself and pull the shirt down farther. She's so damn sweet. I fucking love it.

"You don't want me to see your pussy, sweetheart?" I tease her as my hands land on the outsides of her thighs and slip up her shirt.

Her eyes widen, and I guess she's just now realizing that she's not wearing any underwear.

"You weren't worried about that last night." Her head falls back slightly as she props herself up on her elbows with her eyes closed.

"Mmm. I remember." Her words stop me short of slipping my hands up and onto her bare hips.

"What do you remember, sweetheart?" I ask her in a whisper, trying to keep the anxiety out of my voice. She smiles brightly, but turns her head to avoid my gaze and rolls her eyes. It eases some of my worry, but I want to hear her tell me exactly what she remembers.

"Tell me," I command.

She bites her bottom lip and rocks her hips a little. "You." Her eyes go down to her waist. "Doing that."

"Eating you out?" That blush that suddenly appears on

her cheeks is adorable. She nods her head, not losing any eye contact. I push the shirt up her body and she gasps as I pull her ass closer to me. "What else do you remember, baby?" Fuck, I'm so hard, remembering the taste of her on my tongue. I look down between her thighs and her lips are glistening with arousal. Fuck yes! I'm definitely getting in that pussy. My cock starts leaking and begs to be buried inside her.

"I remember... tasting you."

"You sucked my dick." I focus my eyes on her. "Say it."

Her lips part and her breathing quickens. Yeah, she wants me. And this time it's going to go down like it should've last night.

"I sucked your dick."

"Yeah you did, and you're going to do it again after I cum in this pussy." I smack her pussy hard enough to make her jump. "You're going to lick me clean, aren't you, my dirty girl?"

I watch as her pussy clenches around nothing. She's so fucking turned on right now. I dip my fingers into her heat and curl up to hit that sweet spot.

"Oh!" She falls back on the mattress and her back arches. I smirk at her. I forgot how damn responsive she is. She's too fucking good. I keep pumping my fingers in and out of her quickly, but I keep my pumps shallow, focusing on that sweet spot. I just want to get her off real quick to soften her up. "Get wet for me, Elle."

My words send her off and she trembles beneath me with

the sexiest moan coming from her lips. I feel her cum on my fingers and quickly pull them out and shove my pants down. I take them off and toss them to the floor. She's panting with her head turned to the side. And then just as I line my dick up, she does the same thing as last night. She closes her legs and pushes away from me.

"What's wrong, sweetheart?" I don't understand the look she's giving me. "You want me to grab a condom?"

She clears her throat a little before settling back down on the bed and relaxing slightly. "Umm..." Her blue eyes find mine and she continues. "I don't know."

"I'll get one, sweetheart. It's alright." I move to get off the bed but she pops up and grabs my forearm to stop me.

"No!" she yells out, a little too loud, and seems to be embarrassed by her own reaction.

I give her a questioning look. "I don't mind. I'm clean. So if you're good, I'm good. But I can get one."

She gives me a small smile and then settles back down, releasing my arm. "No, don't." She swallows and opens her legs for me.

Her submission is fucking beautiful. I don't waste any time and settle in between her hips, lining my cock up. Her eyes close, and her head turns to the side as her breathing picks up.

"Uh-uh, sweetheart." Her eyes open. "I want you to look at me while I'm fucking you."

Her mouth parts, and I can feel her pussy clamping down

on the very tip of my dick. I can't believe how turned on she is even though she's already cum. I grip her hips with both hands, tilting her just right and slam into her heat.

Holy fuck, she's so fucking tight. She's strangling my dick. Her head pushes into the mattress and her mouth opens for a silent scream. Her pussy pulses around me as the head of my cock pushes against her cervix.

"You alright, babe?" I have to ask, because she looks lost in a mix of pleasure and pain. But closer to the side of pain, and that's not what I want.

I rub her clit with the rough pad of my thumb and wait for her walls to loosen around me. I rock in and out with shallow strokes and feel her moisture pull between us.

"Yeah." Her head turns to the side, but she keeps her eyes on me. "More," she pants with half-lidded eyes, and I fucking love it. Her lust and pleasure are evident. Thank fuck. I almost thought I was too much for her.

I watch as a cold sweat breaks out on her skin and I lean down, pushing my cock even deeper and kiss her jaw. I feel her body start to shake and her breathing pause, and I know she's close again so soon. I fucking love how easy it is to get her off. I pinch her clit to push her over the edge. Her eyes are dazed as she thrashes under me, cumming on my dick. Her tight walls try to milk my dick, but I'm not even close to being done with her.

"Look at me while you cum." She obeys immediately, and I'm half-surprised she's still so coherent. I wrap my hand around her throat and start pumping her with deep strokes. She's so wet, making my movements easy. I pound her pussy again and again, each stroke harder than the previous, and love the moans of pleasure I force out of her mouth. She moans my name and struggles to keep her eyes on me as her body trembles. Fuck yes. I want another. "Cum for me." And she does. Three fucking times already.

I feel like a king. Her king. I'm her entire world right now. I rule over her body. I *own* her. The thought has me rutting recklessly between her legs. She lets out a strangled cry, and I keep up my pace. My balls draw up and my spine tingles. YES!

I keep my eyes on her as I tilt my hips so each thrust smacks against her clit. I pound into her heat without any mercy, and as soon as I hear her scream my name in complete ecstasy as her body bows with her release, I cum deep inside her heat. She's still so damn tight that our combined cum leaks out from her pussy and down my thighs. I push as far in as I can and love the wet smacking noises I'm making with my deep, hard thrusts.

Waves of heat and pleasure roll through my body. YES! So fucking good. I close my eyes as her body relaxes and just enjoy this moment. Our heavy pants are the only thing I can hear. I fucking love it.

I open my eyes and find her watching me, as though she's waiting for my approval. Such a sweet submissive. I lean down, slipping out of her and let the cum drip on the sheets.

I don't care. I'll wash them after I take her home.

The thought of taking her home hits me as my lips gently brush against hers. I kiss her with more passion than I've ever kissed a woman. I hate that this is the first and the last time.

She kisses me back with the same intensity and I know it's real. This broad can't hide shit from me. I break our kiss and smile down at her.

She winces as I move from between her legs and she closes them.

I look down and see a wet spot on the white sheets crumpled up under us and it's pink. Ah, damn. It's a good thing I didn't go down on her with her time of the month coming.

I slide off the bed and quickly grab a washcloth from the en suite and wet it with warm water.

When I get back to the bed, she's still laying on her side, exhausted and trembling from the aftershocks of her multiple orgasms.

"Open your legs for me, sweetheart." She turns onto her back with her eyes closed and winces as I wipe her off.

My poor sweet girl. I know I was rough, but I didn't think I was *that* rough. She is tight though. I wasn't expecting that.

"You alright sweetheart?" I ask and kiss her cheek.

"Mm hm," she says, nodding her head.

"You sure?" I bend down and kiss her thigh that's still shaking slightly and then her hip.

She shakes her head no. "It's a good hurt."

CHAPTER 11

VINCE

I watch her move in the shower, her hands moving over her skin as she lathers up her body. I'd get in there with her and fuck her against the wall, but she's too sore. I feel like a prick for being so rough. Every time she looks at me she smiles sweetly, so she can't be hurting too bad.

"You sure you don't want to go out for lunch?" I raise my voice enough that she'll be able to hear it over the sound of the water. She didn't eat anything for breakfast; I should at least take her to lunch.

She sighs heavily. "My mom wants me to go home. She thinks I'm mad at her."

"Aren't you?" She *should* be mad at her.

"Yes. But I don't want her to feel bad." I rub my jaw,

deciding on how involved I want to get with this. Fuck it. She's too sweet to watch her being used like that.

"Tell me what happened." She stops washing her hair and looks at me with surprise. "I wanna know."

She goes back to doing her thing and sighs. I almost have to get up to spank that ass for ignoring me, but then she starts talking. "She likes to move around and latch onto men. As long as I can remember, it's what she does." She rinses her hair and the lather washes down her curves. Her nipples are hard and it takes everything in me not to go to her. I want her again so fucking bad. I have to concentrate on how she couldn't walk straight. She's too fucking sore.

If I'd known that would have happened, I would've gone easy, so I could have her again.

"She always picks losers who are drunks like her or have some sort of problem." My eyes snap up to her face and I have to try to remember what the fuck she's talking about. Oh yeah, her mom.

"So what's this guy's deal?" I ask.

"Well, Patrick is a gambler and lost his house because of it. So my sweet mother bought them one after a whopping two months of chatting online."

I huff a laugh. "And now what? She needs you 'cause he lost this one?"

"Yeah, that, and my name's on it."

"What?" All humor leaves me and I lean forward on the

bench. Anger rises in my blood. That's fucked up. I don't know why I feel so defensive, but I do. No mother should do that kind of shit to their daughter. "Are you serious?"

"Yeah, she forged my name on the paperwork. Luckily, whatever bet he made he couldn't use the house as collateral, but she drained her bank account bailing him out, and now I have to come save the day."

"You don't *have* to do a damn thing." It takes a moment for her to look at me. "Except get your name off that mortgage."

She watches me for a second and then nods her head. "It's just..." She trails off as she turns off the water and grabs a towel to dry off. I keep my ass planted firmly on the bench so I don't get any more ideas about fucking her. "She's my mom," she finally concludes.

"So?" I ask, like I don't understand. I do, though. I really get the sympathy. But there's a point when you're being used where you have to put your foot down.

"If I don't help her, no one else is there for her."

"There's a reason for that. There's a reason she's alone." I say.

"I don't want her to be alone though. I want her to be happy." She sounds so sad.

"That's real sweet of you, babe, but sometimes you have to stop letting people use you."

She shifts uncomfortably and then sits down on the bench next to me. I grin when I see her mouth open, and her eyes close in ecstasy. She likes that little hint of pain and I'm pretty sure her clit is still throbbing, priming her for my dick again.

"Vince?" Her tone is off and I don't like it.

"Yeah, sweetheart?" I keep my tone neutral until I can figure out what's wrong this time.

"I was just wondering what all this means to you."

Oh. Fuck. It's one of *those* conversations. I'm not too sure how I want to answer that. So I play dumb. "What do you mean?"

"What's going on between us?" I know it takes a lot for her to be so straightforward, and I respect that.

"We're having fun, babe." The sadness that swarms in her eyes fucking kills me. I have to admit I want to keep seeing this girl. I really want to do all sorts of things to her body. I'd love to test her responsiveness, but it wouldn't be smart. I run my hand through my hair. Fucking her this morning wasn't smart either.

Her eyes fall to the floor, but she nods her head slightly. "I like just having fun. No strings or anything, that's okay," she says. I can see she's hurt and that she wants more. She's just saying what she thinks I want to hear. It tears me up inside.

"You sure you don't want to go to lunch, sweetheart?" I pull her to sit on my lap, still wrapped in her towel. "I'll take you wherever you wanna go." Just one more moment with her, before I have to say goodbye.

She gives me a forced smile and shakes her head. "That's alright. You don't have to do that." Fuck she looks so sad.

Like it's just a pity date.

"I don't have to. I want to." I don't realize how true the words are until they leave my lips.

"I have to get back." She pushes off of me and reaches for the bag of clothes from Neiman Marcus and turns her back to me as she begins to get dressed. I know she's upset, and it hurts.

I wish I could tell her I'll see her tonight, but I'm not fucking inviting her to dinner. I've got one of her textbooks downstairs and I'll text her later tonight to swing by and come pick it up at my parents' house. That way Pops sees her, and I don't get my sweetheart wrapped up with my Ma. That shit's not happening. Ma will have all sorts of ideas going through her head if I bring her home.

"Take your time." I give her a small smile that grows as she turns and smiles back at me. She's not that upset. Something's off, but she knew what this was. I take a few steps towards her and kiss the crook of her neck. Her hand comes around the back of my head to hold me there and I admonish her by nipping her earlobe.

"I'll see you downstairs." She bites her bottom lip and nods with that blush staining her cheeks.

"You alright, sweetheart?" She's been quiet since she came downstairs, even after we left my place. Maybe the high that was keeping the regret from her is wearing off. I don't know what it is. But her sweet smiles are gone now. I hope her memory isn't coming back to her. Seeing her anything but happy makes me nervous and uneasy.

"Yeah, I'm fine." she answers with a forced upbeat in her voice.

"It was fun hanging out with you." I rest my hand on her thigh. We're parked in front of a decent enough house in an average neighborhood.

"Yeah," she says. Her smile falls and she noticeably swallows. "It was fun for me, too." My heart drops looking at the sadness in her eyes. I don't get it. I don't understand why she's so upset.

That's a fucking lie. I know she wants more. But she can't have it. It's over between us. It's better this way. She can't be coming around after the shit she saw. Even though she forgot, I'm not bringing her around the *familia*. I can't.

For fuck's sake, I want her, too. But I can't have her.

Her small hand grips the handle to leave before I can get out of the car. That's not happening. "I'll walk you up." I don't give her a moment to respond. I'm out and around to her side before she can swing the door fully open. I offer her my hand, but she's hesitant to accept. Finally, she does. She gracefully steps out and we walk in silence.

This fucking sucks. I don't know if I want her more because I can't have her, or if what I'm feeling is more than that. It doesn't fucking matter though.

I can't have her, and I need to end this in a way that she knows that. She turns to face me as we get to her door.

But I can't go through with it. Her wide blue eyes focus on me and I find myself leaning forward and wrapping my arms around her waist. She moans into my mouth and kisses me back.

I shouldn't be doing this.

My tongue dips inside, tasting her. My hands find her ass and grip her cheeks. She pulls away from me. Her breathing comes in pants. She wants me. I nip her bottom lip and give her one more kiss.

I may not be able to see her after tonight. But I'm not going to crush her heart until I absolutely have to. I don't want to see her sad. I don't want her angry at me. Not like she was. I fucking love this side of her. I love that she wants me.

"See you later, sweetheart."

She hums in satisfaction and watches me as I walk to the car.

I wait to leave until after she's in the house.

I've gotta get some shit done and then I'll send her a text. My heart hardens in my chest. The *familia* comes to Sunday dinner. I don't want her around them. I know by now everyone will know. An intense urge to protect her makes my muscles tight as I drive away.

I'll just show them she's fine. Let her wait in the foyer or something where they can see her. Then she can go.

And then I'll really have to say goodbye.

CHAPTER 12

ELLE

"I said I'm sorry, Elle."

I hear my mom's voice, but I ignore her as I look through the bills again. I can't fucking believe this.

"I can't afford this!" I yell, interrupting whatever she was about to say. I'm sitting at my desk chair, and I finally turn to look at her. She's pale and gaunt looking. She hasn't taken care of herself. Not recently. Not ever. And it's noticeable. Her blonde hair is pulled tight into a ponytail which makes her skin look even more wrinkled and her face more sunken in. I don't even recognize her.

"Of course you can. They wouldn't let me take out the loans if you couldn't afford them."

"No! I can't!" I can't help the anger heating my blood. I'm going to have to drop out of school. There's no way I can afford to live on a grad student's wage and only work part-time in the lab in order to pay this shit off. My heart sinks in my chest. I shouldn't have to. I shouldn't have to do this.

"How many more?" I ask her. She's done this shit before. I know she's hiding some. Ones that she isn't *that* overdue on.

"Those are the only ones with your name on them." Her eyes widen as she puts her hand over her heart. Her voice lowers as she cries. "I only did it because I had to."

"You didn't *have* to do it!" I'm still angry and still screaming, and that's not what she expects. I can't help it though. It's so true. "You don't have to make my life hell."

She shakes her head and starts to speak, but I stop her.

"Don't! Don't you dare. I'm going to have to quit school now. You know that?" Oddly enough though, quitting school seems like more a relief than anything else.

"You have to know I didn't mean for this to happen. I promise you, Elle. I'm going to fix this. I kicked him out. I did. It was stupid of me. I'm going to my AA meetings, I swear!"

Her eyes plead with me to forgive her as her hands clasp in front of her and tears fall down her face. It melts my anger and just makes me sad. I feel pathetic believing her, but I really do. I can help her. I know I can.

"I'll figure this out, Mom."

She practically runs to me and wraps her arms around my

shoulders, crying as she says thank you and sorry over and over again. I pat her back and try to comfort her until I can send her away.

I stare at the closed door and feel sick to my stomach. She hasn't paid a single dime on the mortgage. So there's a couple grand that I owe there. But what's even worse are the credit cards. Cash withdrawals of thousands of dollars at 22%. I'll consolidate. I don't know who's going to give me a loan for that amount. But I'll find a way. I sift through the papers and mentally calculate what I need. A little over 26k in total. My heart sinks. I made 22k a year at my old college, and a measly 14k being the night shift part-timer in the lab. I have nothing saved up because of her last "situation". And I make 26k at this university and haven't found a job here yet.

My head falls into my hands. There's just no way. I don't see how anyone would loan me the money.

I'll try. The least I can do is try. I stand up from the desk and breathe in deep. I'm not going to cry because that accomplishes nothing.

I take one step and wince. I can still feel him inside of me. I feel raw and sore, but I love it. It's a strange feeling, finally giving myself to someone.

I shake my head and sigh as I lay down on the bed. It's not even made. All my stuff is still in moving boxes, along with my sheets. I don't have much. But it'll feel better once this room looks like my old bedroom.

I close my eyes and remember his hands on me. The heated looks he gave me as he fucked me. I moan and clench my thighs, loving the soreness. I want him again and again. I loved the way he fucked me. I've really been missing out.

I pop up and and dig in my purse for the birth control pills. It's a few hours late, but it'll be alright. I bite the inside of my cheek. Maybe I should get the morning after pill too. I feel my cheeks flame and I start feeling ... dirty. I don't like the tightness in my chest. I wanted the whole experience and I got it. Maybe I'm naïve or stupid. I don't know, maybe I'm a slut for wanting that. I swallow the lump in my throat and grab my bottle of water to swallow down the pill. It doesn't matter now. I got what I wanted.

My heart hurts. I don't know what to think. One moment he's noncommittal, the next he's kissing me like he needs the air in my lungs to breathe.

I understand it probably seemed like a hookup last night, but I can't help wanting more.

I roll my eyes. Of course I'm being a clingy bitch. No man wants that. And that's not what this was. It may have felt like more to me, but I'm sure that's only because he was my first. I wonder if I told him that last night. I'm too embarrassed to ask. I pick up my phone and scroll through the contacts. Before we left he called himself from my phone so he'd have my number. I like that. I like how in charge he is. My eyes widen as I look at the screen and see it light up with a text from him.

Shit! I didn't press send or anything, did I? I stare at it for a moment trying to figure out what the hell I did before I realize he's the one who sent me a text. My heart beats rapidly and I find my body heating with nerves.

What the hell? I feel like I'm in high school again. I calm my nerves and realize the reason he's texting is just that I've left one of my textbooks back at his place.

That was stupid of me. Also... I'm gonna need that so I can sell it. These books aren't cheap.

As I'm debating how to reply, another text comes through:

Meet me at my parents' house, it's closer to you and I'll be there tonight at 5.

The text is followed up with an address. I wonder if I should wait a few minutes before responding, but I'm pretty sure he can see that I've read them anyway. I cringe. I wonder if that looks clingy. I don't want to look that way. I wanna seem laid-back. Eh. Whatever. I shrug my shoulder and send a reply.

Thanks. I'll see you then.

And thanks for the orgasms this morning. May I have another? I laugh at my inner thought. I am not sending that, although it's exactly what I want to say. He's sweet and funny. And fucks my body like it was made for his dick. My thighs clench again.

Damn, one time and I'm a sex addict. I put down my phone and sit up, ready to get my mind on something else. But then I remember the shit my mother left me saddled with, and my heart sinks. I bite the inside of my cheek. I need to get my ass up and go look for a job. Make that jobs. One for myself, and one fit for a recovering alcoholic. I'm not going to waste my life taking care of her. She needs to get her shit in order. I nod my head with anger as I pull my laptop from my bag and open it up on the desk.

Everything's going to be just fine. Even as I think the words and try to believe them, something deep in my gut is telling me it's a lie.

CHAPTER 13

VINCE

I put the phone back in my pocket. She's quick to answer and agreed to meet me tonight, just like I knew my sweetheart would. She's giving me a clingy vibe--usually that turns me off, but on her, I like it.

I blow out a long exhale and face the docks. If only the rest of my day could be this easy.

"Boss, we got another problem." Tommy walks up behind me. I turn to look at him and see his chin is bruised up nice. Seeing it almost makes me feel like a prick. Almost. I know he was doing what he thought was best for the family, but fuck that. I'd do it again if I had to.

"It's all fucked today." I shove my hands in my pockets

and stare at the water, listening to the waves beat against the dock. Three orders came in, but all three were only partially filled. "What's wrong with this one?"

"Supposed to be 50 pounds." I nod my head. I know how much we should be getting from the Marzano Cartel. It's the same we've been getting for nearly 7 months now. "We've only got 42 here."

"Someone is skimming. Who is it that counted? I want all the names, Tommy."

"I was there for this one, boss. I saw it opened."

"And the container?" It's possible someone fucked with them on the ship. In which case we have all their names and addresses. Someone would have a real rough night if it came down to that.

"Locked and untouched." He's confident, and that tells me everything I need to know.

"So it's their end that's fucking with us." That's not good. It's never good ending business relations in the line of work we do. But I'm not putting up with this shit. "Did they think we wouldn't notice 8 pounds were missing?" Not to mention the guns. They were light, too.

"Could be someone in packing on their end." Tommy's got a point.

"I'll send a message to Javier. We need this shit dealt with immediately." I have to walk back to the docks to get the phone we use for that shit. Tommy walks with me.

"How's the other situation going?" he asks. My hands flex and I crack my neck trying to keep my temper at bay. I know he's concerned, but I don't like him asking about her.

"It worked. She doesn't remember shit."

He nods his head and grins. "That's fucking fantastic." He doesn't sound as thrilled as he'd like me to believe he is. "You sure about that?"

"Positive." He shuts his mouth and nods his head, walking silently beside me. I'm the underboss, he knows not to question me. I can see his worry though, so I decide to put him out of his misery. "She's easy to read, and she's gonna come over tonight for a quick second to grab a book I took from her." I open the heavy door and grin at him. "You can see for yourself, Tommy."

"So what'd she think? You two just had a wild night together?"

I give him a smug look that lets him know that's exactly what she thought and that I got some this morning too.

"Are you fucking for real? You tapped that ass?" He's grinning from ear to ear, but shaking his head in disbelief.

"Damn right." I hesitate to say more, but I figure why the hell not let him in on it. "I want her again, too."

He cocks an eyebrow at me. "Going back for seconds isn't your thing."

"Wasn't. But this girl is real sweet." I don't usually brag, but this broad is different. I want everyone to know I had her.

More than that, I want them to know she's mine.

"Good girls like bad boys. I want me one of those." He says.

"A good girl?" I ask.

"Yeah."

"Then go get one." I park my ass at my desk and unlock the desk drawer. I reach in and grab the right cell phone and flip through the info on my notepad. I appreciate Tommy's distraction, 'cause this shit fucking sucks.

"They aren't all that easy to find, not with how often you've got me working." He sits at one of the opposite seats and stretches his legs out in front of him. He nervously runs his hand on the back of his neck and opens and shuts his mouth a few times.

"What's going on?" I just want him to say whatever the fuck is on his mind.

He spits it out without the need for further prodding. "I'm real fucking sorry, Vince." His eyes turn sad. "You know I didn't want to. I was just doing things according to protocol."

I look him directly in the eye. "Witnesses don't live to be witnesses." That's still protocol. It was stupid of me to risk this shit. Everyone knows it. I worry a bit that they think women make me soft. Specifically, this woman. After all, I'm going to be the one taking over. I can't have them thinking that. "This was a one-off, Tommy. You did what you should've."

"Alright boss." He taps his hands on the armrests and looks like he's getting ready to take off.

"Everything else good for going out tonight?" I ask him, while I have his attention.

"Everything is set. Unless you want to add anything in the shipment going to the cartel."

I smirk at him. "Not yet, let's make sure we play this smart." Sending a message like what he's thinking would be bad for everyone. I gotta make this call and let our business partners know what's up. Eight pounds missing is over 200 grand of our money gone, but it's over a million in gross after it's cut and sold. Whoever took it wanted a reaction from us. They're going to get one. I just have to figure out exactly who it was that tried to fuck us over and what they thought they'd get from pulling this shit. Stealing some product to profit on the side is one thing. Skimming off the top--I've seen that, too.

But fucking with a shipment to start a war is also a possibility. The thought gives me an uneasy feeling. War is something we've dealt with not too long ago, with my brother Dom. And his woman got caught up in that shit. An uneasy feeling settles in my gut. I'm not gonna let that shit happen again.

CHAPTER 14

ELLE

I'm feeling more and more pathetic as I scroll through my phone. I literally have no one to talk to. I want to tell someone that I lost my V-card. *Anyone.* But I feel a bit pathetic that it took me this long, and who am I going to talk to anyway? I just realized I've essentially lost touch with all my friends from undergrad. We like each other's FB posts, but I haven't had a real conversation with Michelle or Amy in almost two years. Michelle is married now, and I think she's pregnant. Yeah, she's definitely pregnant. I remember seeing a picture of her with a huge belly, opening a box of blue balloons. Damn. I'm really out of touch.

That's alright though. I'm going to start today. After

all, I need to meet people in this town so that I can find a job. I applied for 20 positions, everything from waitressing and working at the hardware store, to working as a library assistant at the university. I'm almost out of gas now, too. I picked up a few applications for Mom, but she needs to get her shit together first.

The more I think about it, the more I realize I need to get mom to just sell this house. I can get a part-time job and still go to school, just like I did back in Maryland. I can do it again here. Only this time I'll have Mom live with me so I can keep an eye on her.

I shove my phone into my clutch and take a look at myself in the dresser mirror. I have to back up and stand on my tiptoes to see my outfit fully. I like it. I think I look pretty in this yellow and white, striped cotton sundress, but still laid-back. The dress flows out from my hips in an A-line shape, but hugs the little dip in my waist. If only my boobs were bigger. I scrunch my nose wondering if I should grab my padded bra. My lips purse as I decide no, I don't need that. He knows they're little. It's too late to fool him now.

I'm guessing he just wants me to run in and grab the book, which is fine. I want to look good though. *And* I'm not going to be clingy or anything like that. I'm going to play it cool. He doesn't want strings, and I get that. I don't need strings or a commitment. It's not like I have my shit together anyway. But I don't like the idea of it being just a fling.

I'm sure that's what I was thinking last night, trying to hook up with him. I bet I took an extra shot or two so I'd have the courage to go through with it this time. It's not like I've been saving myself. I just haven't gotten around to it.

Each step down the stairs makes the soreness between my legs obvious. I can't hide from what I did. Part of me is feeling ashamed. Like I should have saved myself for someone who would've loved me. But I keep shoving that feeling down. My father never loved my mother. Most of my friends growing up were the products of divorced parents. Love is something that comes and goes, I suppose. I don't know if I'll ever even fall in love. I don't know if I have it in me.

But a quick fuck with no strings attached was something I thought I could handle. I always chickened out though. I'm not sure if I was more afraid that I'd fall for the guy and get hurt, or that I would be sorely disappointed afterward. I wince at the bottom step and try to bend down to relieve some of the ache between my thighs. So far, so good on both fronts, although the possibility of falling for Vince is high on my list. A sexy man who knows how to fuck, with his own house and an adorable puppy? Yes, please! But there's always a catch. So I'm going to hold back. I'm not going to put my heart out there to be stomped. And everything is going to be just fine.

I look straight ahead and see my mother passed out on the couch. I close my eyes and take a deep breath to calm myself. It will all be fine. Everything will be fine. I walk over to her and brush the hair out of her face. One of her arms is hanging off of the side of the sofa and she's drooling on a pillow. She doesn't even have any pants on. Just a saggy old tank top and her underwear.

I bet if I looked in the kitchen, I'd find the bottle. I lean down closer and smell gin on her breath. Tears prick at my eyes. How can she keep doing this to herself? And to me, too? I spent all afternoon searching for a job while she got drunk. Deep down I know I can't stand for this. I need to do something. I just don't know what. I don't know how to say no to her without hurting her. And more than anything else, I don't want to hurt her. I put a hand on my heart and try to relieve the ache. My throat dries up, and I will the emotions away.

I'll go to AA with her. I will help her like a daughter should.

I take a step away and reach down for my keys, and I hear her mumble my name.

"It's your fault he hates me." I barely make out the words she speaks in her sleep.

I know what she's talking about. It's not the first time I've heard it either. I was the mistake that ruined my mother's chances at a real life. At least that's what she says when she's drunk. Angry drunk perfectly describes my Mom. But I'm going to help her.

I'm extremely quiet on my way out. I haven't lived here long enough to know where all the creaks in the floorboards are just yet. I wish I knew though, so I could make sure to avoid them as I leave. I don't want to wake her up. Not when she's thinking those thoughts. I don't want to get into another fight with her. Not over that. I don't even breathe until I've shut the door.

I twist the handle as I shut the door to avoid the loud click it would make otherwise, and then lock it. When I turn around, I lean back against the door for a moment. I take a deep breath, and my eyes catch sight of a plain, white car. It looks old and I've never seen it before. It's really out of place parked on the opposite side of the street. I see two women sitting in the front seats, each on their phones and any anxiety I had about the car is washed away.

I try to remember what I'm supposed to be doing. What I was so scared to hope for.

Vince.

I shake my head and feel stupid for even thinking about him. He's just giving me the book back. It was just a fling. I get in my car and look at my makeup. This is all so pointless and stupid. Just like this dress.

He's just going to give me the book, and then I'll leave. I'll probably never even hear from him again. That would be best anyway.

CHAPTER 15

VINCE

"How much is gone?" Dom asks as soon as I walk in the dining room. Becca's in the backyard picking basil leaves or some shit. And she's getting big. She looks like she's going to pop any day now even though they've got a few months left before their little one is supposed to be here. Apparently I'm an asshole for saying that. Next time I'll keep my mouth shut or say she's glowing or some shit like that. The kids are with Ma and Anthony. So it's just Tommy, Pops, Dom, and Becca for now, and everyone else will show up later. No one ever misses Ma's Sunday dinners.

"We're off by about half a mil on this shipment." I answer him and Dom's eyes go wide, then the anger settles in.

"You've gotta be fucking kidding me." He's pissed. He's "lying low" with his fancy professor job, but he's still in charge of the money. I knew he wouldn't want to hear this shit.

"It's a setup for sure." I say.

"The cartel?" he asks.

"No. Javier had no clue. Said everything is monitored and would check it out. Right now I'm just waiting to hear back, but my money is on someone in packing. Someone with connections here who wants the territory."

"Who's trying to fuck with us? You think it's Shadows MC?" Dom's stayed in the loop more than I thought he would've. Shadows Motorcycle Club has been itching for territory, but I don't see them pulling the trigger. We'd easily take them out. No one that I can think of has been wanting to fuck with us.

"We'll find out once I hear back from Javier with a name."

"What about the money?" He asks.

I frown and I suppress a groan. "They're waiting to make sure it's on their end, and then we'll talk."

"Best for business relations I guess." Irritation colors his voice, but he's right. I fucking hate waiting though.

Thinking about waiting reminds me that my sweetheart should be here soon. I have a bit of anxiety over her coming here. I'm worried something's gonna set someone off. I just want her in and out. And then on my dick again. I can't help that last part. My stomach knots thinking about how I'm gonna have to end it. I don't fucking want to though.

Tommy comes into the room and he must read my mind, or see me shifting my hardening dick in my pants. He busts out a laugh from his gut. "Your girl staying for dinner, Vince?"

"Girl? Since when did you settle down?" The look of approval in Dom's eyes makes me want to smack it away. I didn't settle, and I'm not settling down.

"I didn't, and I'm not. A broad's coming by to pick something up so Pops can see her and then she's gone."

"Thought you wanted to see her again?" Tommy asks.

"I do, but that'd be stupid."

"What's stupid is not taking something you want." Dom starts and I'm quick to cut him off.

"It's done, Dom. I can't have her, and I won't. I'm ending it as soon as she gets here." The absolution is firm in my voice, but I don't want it.

"What's wrong with her?" Dom asks, and it makes me angry. Not a damn thing is wrong with her.

"She's a witness, that's what's wrong," Pops says as he comes into the room, and Dom seems confused for a moment, but then pissed. Calling her a witness makes my blood run cold.

"A witness to what?" Dom asks.

"Doesn't fucking matter, because she doesn't remember shit," I say, putting an end to the conversation. "She's not a witness." My words come out hard and everyone looks at me like they'd like to disagree, but they're smart enough to keep their mouths shut. "Pops just wants to be sure. And

I'm gonna show him she's good, and then she walks. No one fucking touches her."

Dom's eyebrows raise and I stare at him until he concedes. "Whatever you say, Vince." He throws up his hands in surrender. "I don't have a problem with it if you say it's all good." Pops nods his head and slaps a hand on my shoulder.

Before he can speak the doorbell rings, and we all look at the door. My heart clenches, knowing I'm gonna be saying goodbye to my sweetheart. It's going to break her heart, but she shouldn't be with a man like me anyway.

She's too good for me. I'm sure she knows that.

I walk quickly to the door, knowing the book is on the dining room table. I'll walk her in so everyone can see her, and walk her ass right back out.

Nice and easy.

My chest tightens as I twist the doorknob. I'm not sure if it's because I think something's going to go wrong, or because I won't be able to let go.

Chapter 16

Vince

She looks beautiful in her little dress. I like it more than those tiny-ass shorts she was wearing when we first met. She looks like the sweetheart she is. That, and no one can see how perky her ass is in this dress. She should wear dresses like this all the time. I give her a tight smile even though seeing her puts me a bit at ease. My nerves are fucking killing me. I swear to God everyone can hear how fast my heart's beating.

I need to get my shit together. Everything's gonna be fine. And then I'll end this, and she'll be safe. My heart drops in my chest knowing she won't be mine. She'll never be mine. But at least I know she'll be safe.

"Come on in, sweetheart," I greet her, and open the door

good and wide for her to enter. My parents' house is a nice home, but it's old. Family pictures line the wall of the foyer. All of the picture frames are different, and there are a couple dozen of them in total. Ma doesn't like taking any photos down, just adding new ones over time. The newest are the pictures of my nephew, Ethan. Dom's little boy looks just like him.

She smiles, but it seems just as forced as mine. My heart sputters in my chest. She didn't remember, did she? Her eyes linger on the pictures, and her lips soften and pull into a genuine smile. Good. I want her to be happy. I want them to see how happy and at ease she is. My eyes focus past her and land on Tommy. If she remembered what she witnessed yesterday, there's no way she'd be alright in front of him.

She turns, and the dress flutters out at the motion. Her ponytail sways back and forth in time with her hips. My eyes focus on those hips. I want to flip up her dress and fuck the shit out of her. The need to claim her is riding me hard, but I need to shake that shit off.

"Hi there, beautiful," Tommy says to her as she walks into the dining room, making a beeline for the book that's on the edge of the table. I don't like his tone. I know he's just testing her, but I don't like him calling her beautiful.

"Hi there," she answers in a peppy voice and grabs her book, hugging it to her chest. The pressure makes her breasts bulge slightly from the top of the sweetheart neckline of her dress and gives them a fuller look. She's not doing it on purpose, but I wanna spank her ass for it all the same.

Fuck this broad has gotten under my skin. All I can think about is nailing her, but now is not the time or place.

"How are you doing? Elle, is it?" Pops asks. He's across the room still, pouring himself a scotch from the old bar in the corner of the room.

"I'll take one of those, Pops," I say over Elle as she starts to answer him, and feel like an ass for interrupting. My nerves are getting to me and this isn't good. The *familia's* here. Pops is here. I need to get my shit together and keep it cool. I can't fuck this up. "Sorry, sweetheart." I gentle my hand on the small of her back and give her a kiss on the cheek. "Elle, that's my Pops, my cousin Tommy, and my brother Dom." They nod at her in turn as I introduce them one by one. "Dom's wife Becca is out back."

"Hi everyone." She looks timid and shy, and rocks a little on her heels before turning to me. "Thank you for this." Her big blue eyes meet mine and I can't speak. I don't want to walk her to the door and say goodbye.

"No problem," I finally answer, and then clear my throat. I turn, ready to walk her out, but Pops' voice bellows from across the room.

"So, how'd you two meet?" he asks.

I meet his gaze as Elle answers. I wish he wouldn't do this shit. "At a bar last night, I left my book," a blush rises in her cheeks, "in Vince's car." Her shoulders hunch inward and she fidgets with one of her heels on the ground. She's a fucking horrible liar. "He was nice enough to take me home. I drank a little too much." She can't even look Pops in the eyes. A chuckle rises up my chest and I can't stop it. She looks at me with wide, pleading eyes. She's fucking adorable.

"No problem, sweetheart." I turn my body again to lead her out. I know it's rude to be ending it so short, and I can see the hurt in her eyes, but it's for the best.

"You don't want to stay for dinner?" Dom asks, and I want to beat the shit out of him for it.

"No--"

"No--" We both answer at the same time, and then exchange glances. Why the fuck doesn't she want to stay for dinner? My eyes narrow on hers searching for an answer. I mean it's not like I invited her, but still. She's fucking quick to get out of here. She breaks my gaze and turns to walk towards the door.

She smiles over her shoulder, still holding the book like it's her lifeline. "Nice to meet you all."

"I'll walk you out, sweetheart." I open the door for her and place my hand on her back.

"That's alright," she replies, and her tone is sad. "It's fine."

The way she says it's fine makes it obvious that she's not fine. "I *want* to walk you out." The words come out of my mouth before I can stop them. I don't like the look on her face. I don't like seeing her so unhappy. But should I walk her out?

No, no I shouldn't. I should let this end already. End it quickly and cleanly. Ignore her texts. That's what I should do.

Her eyes fall to the floor as she gives me a weak smile and relents. "Okay." My heart fucking hurts. I guess she can sense what's going on. Fuck, this sucks.

I open the door all the way and take a step to push the screen door open for her, but a loud bang from the dining room makes both of us jump. Tommy cusses with both of his hands raised, broken glass and bourbon at his feet. Clumsy fuck dropped his glass. I raise my eyes and look around the room as Tommy swears and wipes his hands down the front of his shirt. They focus right on Pops, but his eyes aren't on me. They're on Elle.

Her eyes are wide, and her chest rises and falls dramatically. At first I think the loud bang and Tommy cussing scared her. But this is more. This is bad, really fucking bad. I remember right before she woke up in the office. I grind my teeth in anger. He dropped something then too. The loud bang, him cussing. Fuck! Could it really be triggered that easily? She was almost gone. Almost in the clear. Her feet back up with small steps, pushing the door into the wall. Her knuckles turn white, clutching that damn book.

She swallows thickly and then looks at me. Her eyes dart from me, to each of the men in the room who are all staring at her now. She reaches for the knob to the screen door, and lets out a small scream as I pull it shut and pull her into my chest. I back her ass into my crotch and push the front door closed behind us.

Dom looks at Pops, who says something I can't quite make out. Guessing by how fast Dom takes off through the kitchen to the backyard, it must be about getting to Becca. Sure enough, I hear the sliding doors open and slam closed.

No one moves, and the only sound is Elle crying softly. She shakes her head in my arms and I find myself shushing her. She's not fighting me. But she knows something. She remembered *something*.

"Sweetheart, tell me what's wrong," I say calmly into her ear. She's facing the dining room. Everyone can see her and I hate that, so I turn her in my arms, but she tries to back away from me. She wants to get out of my arms and I don't like that. She's not going anywhere.

"Nothing. Please just let me go."

I give her a small smile and brush the tears off her cheeks. Her skin is so soft. So perfect. "I can't do that now, can I? Something's wrong, and you need to tell me what."

Her breath comes in chaotically as she frantically looks around the room like she's trapped. Which she is.

"Sweetheart, you need to calm down." I try to pet her back to calm her ass down, although I'm not sure what the point of that is.

Tommy comes up to my right side with those fucking pills in his hands, ready to shove them down her throat again.

"No! Get that shit out of her face."

"You sure, Vince?" Fuck. It didn't work. I'm not doing it again. It didn't fucking work.

I look around the room and feel like a failure. I failed my Pops, Tommy, and especially Elle. It's all my fucking fault.

"Please don't hurt me," she whispers.

"What do you remember, babe?" I ask.

"Nothing." She's quick to answer while shaking her head.

"Don't lie to me." My words are cold, and my grip on her tightens. "I've got all night sweetheart, but I'd rather you just tell me now." It hits me in that moment, as I look past her to my Pops, she's dead. Doesn't matter what all she remembers. She's dead.

"I remember," she gasps and holds the book tighter. She tries to speak again, "the woods." I wasn't expecting that.

"What about 'em?" I ask.

"How we," she swallows and keeps her eyes closed tight, "how you." She breathes in deep trying to settles her breath, "took me in the woods."

Oh, fuck that! Anger consumes me and adrenaline rushes through me.

"Took you?" I raise my voice. "As in, fucked you?" She visibly recoils at my anger, and she tries to get out of my arms again. "No, no, sweetheart, that shit did not happen." This is not fucking happening. Her memory comes back and it's some shit that makes me a god damned villain. Something I didn't even do!

"I--" she tries to speak, and then finally meets my eyes. Hers are red-rimmed and filled with tears. "I think I remember."

"Sweetheart, your memory is wrong. We screwed around a bit, but that's not what happened in the woods."

Her eyes look to the wall and then back to me. Her hand raises to her throat. "Did you hurt me?" As she asks, her eyes drift to the faint marks on her wrists, and her eyes widen.

"It's not what you think." I try to keep my voice even, but my skin is on fire and I can feel their eyes boring into me, thinking I hurt her.

"No, we didn't. I know we didn't. This morning was the first time." Her voice is small as she stares at her wrists and then closes her eyes.

"That's right we didn't. I wouldn't fuck you when you were like that."

She raises her eyes to mine. "But you did hurt me. I remember. I remember you, and I remember them. You were angry with me."

Her breath comes in shallow pants and then she looks behind me at Pops and Tommy. She hesitantly steps closer to me, but then looks at the door. "Please let me go. I won't say anything." Her small hand settles on my chest and her eyes plead with me. "Please."

"I can't let that happen, sweetheart." It fucking kills me to say it. I see Tommy leave the room, but my father stays.

"I won't say anything. I don't know what to think. I'm not okay," she says.

"No, you're not okay," I answer back. Truer words have never been said.

She swallows thickly and then looks back at the door again with tears running down her cheeks. "I'm scared, Vince." She's huddling next to me like I'm going to save her.

I tell her the only thing I can think of to say. "You should be."

CHAPTER 17

ELLE

"I don't want to hurt you, sweetheart. I don't want to, but I will." I hear Vince's cold, hard voice in my head over and over again. A chill washes through my body. I push my body into his chest as though it will make it go away. I don't know what's real. My mind is fucking with me.

Flashes of scenes play before my eyes. His handsome smile as he introduces himself to me. *"I'm Vince."* The heated look in his eyes as he looks up at me from between my legs. But then, there's more. More that I didn't remember this morning. Him choking me, pinning me against the wall. Then his cousin and another man. Smaller in size than Vince, but both with threatening looks on their faces. It makes my heart skip a beat.

"Vince, what happened?" I whisper into his chest, afraid to know the answer. But I need something. Something is very, very wrong.

"I can't tell you, sweetheart." His calm voice forces a sob up my throat.

"Please don't hurt me," I beg him. I know he will though. I can sense it in the thick air, in the way they all looked at me. I'm answered with silence. "I'm not supposed to remember, am I?"

"I'm sorry, Elle." His words are more sad than anything else. He's truly remorseful, and that makes me sick to my stomach. He doesn't have to hurt me.

I push the words through my hollow chest. "I promise--"

He cuts me off. "That's not good enough."

"What can I do? Please," I cry into his shirt and drop the book to the floor. I was just with him this morning. "Please, Vince. I swear."

I feel a strong hand on my back and Vince turns his body, taking me with him and pushing my back against the wall.

"Don't fucking touch her," he growls above my head, looking over his shoulder.

My body stills with fear and I can't breathe.

"No one touches her!" he screams above my head.

I grip onto his shirt tighter. He'll save me. He has to save me.

He grips my hip and throws the front door open. "Vince, what are you doing?" It's his father's voice.

"I'm taking her to the cabin." I nearly trip trying to keep

up with him. Everything flies past me in a blur from the tears and from how quickly he moves my body outside to his car.

And then he opens the trunk. My feet dig into the ground, and I try to push away from him, but he picks me up and tosses me in like I weigh nothing. My head bangs against the floor of the trunk and I scream out. When I open my eyes, I see his hard gaze.

"None of that, sweetheart. Be a good girl and stay quiet." I don't dare disobey him. I know he's my only hope.

CHAPTER 18

ELLE

The entire car ride, I'm silent. I close my eyes and try to remember. I think I remember being here before, being tied up. My fingers graze over the faint marks on my wrists. I'm quiet. I'll do as he says for now, but I know that will only get me so far. How the fuck did this happen? I concentrate on breathing and then I remember about a secret latch in the trunk. Well, not secret. But there's a latch in here somewhere. My hands run along every surface looking for it. But there's nothing. I spend the entire ride looking for it, only to come up short.

My breathing hitches the longer the car stays still. My body jolts as the car door slams. A whimper escapes me and I cover my mouth. The light burns my eyes as he opens the trunk. It's not that bright, but compared to the darkness in the trunk, it kills my sight. He reaches in and picks me up easily by my waist. I cower under his touch as he sets me down. My feet land softly, and that's when I remember. Like deja vu.

I remember running.

My eyes follow the path I took. I remember his hard body knocking me to the ground. And then I have flashes of memories of him pounding into me, both of us naked as he ruts between my legs, pushing my body into the dirt.

As if reading my mind, Vince growls out, "I didn't." His tone is defensive and hard. I swallow the lump growing in my throat. I know he didn't. I would have felt it this morning. But I remember it. Why do I remember it happening that way? More importantly, why did he want me to forget?

"I know." The words catch in my throat and come out much higher than I intended. I clear my throat and cross my arms to grip my shoulders. "I don't understand, Vince."

He takes a deep breath, but doesn't meet my eyes. "You need to go inside, Elle."

I look at the house. It's the same country home I thought was so cute this morning, but as I look at it now, fear makes my legs collapse. We're in the middle of nowhere. I can't go in there. In the movies, a secluded place like this is where they kill you. No one will hear me scream. My body begs me to run.

Vince grips my elbow and leans into my neck. His hot breath sends chills down my shoulder and back as he warns,

"Don't you fucking dare run from me."

A whimper escapes my lips. He pulls me toward the house and I move with him. This has happened before, and I was still alive this morning despite everything. Maybe it will happen again.

"Will I forget in the morning?" I can only hope I will.

"No." He swings the front door open as the hope dies in my chest. "It didn't work."

"I don't understand," I plead.

"Stop whining!" he yells at me as I walk inside with him. His anger forces me to rip my arm from his grasp, but it's a clumsy, uncontrolled motion, and my back slams against the wall just inside the door. My hands cover my mouth and I try to stifle the need to cry.

"Fuck!" he screams into the air, and kicks the door. I hear Rigs barking upstairs. His paws scratch against a door. I back away slowly and find myself cowering in the corner. Vince's fists slam into the wall, leaving dents and a trail of blood on the white walls. His knuckles are bloodied but he keeps doing it over and over. Each time his fists pound against the wall my chest jumps and a scream threatens to escape. Rigs barks and growls and Vince yells at him to be quiet.

I'm fucked. I'm so fucked.

He finally stops and takes a deep breath. The only sounds in the room are the dog barking and Vince's heavy breaths. His large shoulders rise and fall with power. He turns slowly towards me and stares at me for a long time. When he finally opens his mouth I let out a heavy breath I didn't realize I was holding. "I'm supposed to kill you," he says.

My body turns weak and I fall to the floor. I want to plead, but I can't. I can't do anything. I'm paralyzed. *I don't want to die.*

"I'm going to figure something out, sweetheart." He walks slowly toward me and picks up my trembling body. Half of me wants to push him off of me and try to run, but the other half is too terrified to consider fighting. The terrified side is the side that is winning. He carries me up the stairs and I remain as still as possible in his arms.

He speaks calmly. "You need to be good for me. You need to make this easy." I can't respond. But if I could, I'd tell him to go fuck himself. I'm not going to make it easy for him to kill me. I can't speak the words, but he must sense my disobedience. "Don't you fuck with me, Elle."

I shouldn't make him angry, but I can't answer. Fear has crippled me.

He kicks a door open, and I recognize the room. It's where we were this morning. I look at the messy bed, still unmade, and see a pink stain on the sheets.

I hear him shushing me; I feel him trying to comfort me. It just makes me feel even worse.

My chest has never felt so hollow or painful before. I never knew I could feel this much physical pain from emotional damage.

CHAPTER 19

VINCE

What the fuck am I going to do? My phone keeps going off in my pocket. I know it's the guys or Pops. I can't answer it. I know what they're going to say. I know their argument. I really believe her, I do. She's not going to say shit. But I can hear them shooting back the next logical question. *What if she remembers more?* I still don't have an answer to that question.

Not only that, but she's been seen with me now. Twice. If someone happened to be watching, which happens every now and then--if they're watching and saw her, they can take her in. They can put pressure on her. And even the best of people collapse under that pressure. I look down at Elle and try rubbing her back again. She's curled up on the bed. They'd get to her for sure. She couldn't tell a lie to save her life.

Rigs barks again and I know my poor pup wants out of the spare bedroom. I left him in there so he wouldn't chew up all the furniture while I was gone. He wants to make sure everything is alright. But it's not. He's gonna have to stay in there until I can calmly let him out. This is so fucked. It's all just fucked.

I try pulling her back to me, closer to me. My hand is fucking killing me, but I need to comfort her. I shouldn't have done that. I know I scared her. Now she won't even look at me. I just want to hold her. But she's scooting away. I don't like it. I don't want to let go of her, but I need to figure this shit out. And realistically, the only thing I can come up with, is that she has to go.

I knew it back at my parents' house. I could see it happening, one of them coming up from behind her with a syringe filled with a lethal injection cocktail trio. It would feel like a pinch, and then it'd be over with. She'd go quickly and painlessly. But the image of her dead and limp in my arms is something I can't handle. I don't want that. I want her to live. I want to see her happy.

I need to figure this shit out, but I haven't got a clue how. We never let witnesses live. I've got nothing but our standard protocol to go on.

I wrap my arms around her waist and pull her to me, forcing her into my lap. Her hand whips out and pushes violently against my chest.

"Don't push me, sweetheart," I grit through my teeth. You'd think she'd be doing whatever she could not to make me angry. I'm her only fucking hope.

"Fuck you!" she screams out, and I grab her mouth to silence her.

"Watch your mouth."

"Don't touch me!" She yells.

"Sweetheart, watch that mouth-"

"Fuck you!" she yells again.

"Oh yeah?" I pin her ass down on the bed. Both of her tiny wrists fit easily in one hand, and I shove them above her head and dig them into the mattress. My hip pins hers down. "You really think you should be talking to me like that, Elle?" I keep the threat in my voice. I have a soft spot for this broad. Everyone's gonna know it. But not her. She can't know that, not yet. She needs to be afraid until I can figure this shit out. And right now, fear is not the dominant emotion that I sense.

"Just kill me!" she screams in my face. Her words hit me like a bullet to the chest. Her face is red and her cheeks are stained with tears. Her eyes glassy with more unshed tears. Her voice lowers. "I know you're going to kill me, so just do it already."

"I don't want to kill you, Elle." It's true. I don't want to. The fact that she's telling me to kill her makes me sick to my stomach.

"So you're going to let me go?" Her voice doesn't hold any hope; she already knows the answer will be no.

"No." She closes her eyes at my answer and turns on

the bed to face away from me as best she can with me still pinning her down. I loosen my grip and let her go. I run a hand down my face and look around the room. It's a safe house. So there's no way she can get out of here. I need to go. I've got to get out of here for just a minute and figure out just how badly I've fucked up. And let my dog out before he tears the door down.

I open the door and check my key in the lock to make sure she can't lock me out. She can't. So that's a plus, I guess. I look back at her lying limp and in the fetal position on the bed. "I'm not going to hurt you." I say it just loud enough for her to hear and take a step out into the hallway.

I shut the door and my fucking heart breaks as I barely make out her words. "You already have."

CHAPTER 20

ELLE

I have no fucking clue where I am. Obviously this is Vince's house, but where this is located, I have no idea. I didn't pay attention this morning either. I just know it was a long drive. But I'm getting out of here. There's no way I'm staying here. I don't know how long he's going to keep me here. I know they want me dead. They can't risk me remembering whatever the fuck it is that I saw. But I really need to get the fuck away from here as fast as I can.

I finally get my ass off the bed and wipe the tears from my face. I need to do *something*. I can't just wait here to die. For all I know he's going to come in the room with a gun or something and kill me, or however the fuck they do it. I can't just wait around. I won't. I don't want to die.

I walk as quietly as I can to the curtains in the room and open them wide. The windows are large. Really fucking large. Like they were meant to be used to escape from the bedroom. Good. 'Cause that's exactly what I'm going to do. I run my hand along the top of the sill, searching for a latch, but I don't find one. My forehead wrinkles with consternation, and my heart beats faster. I push against the top. I try pushing it up with everything I have in me. But it doesn't budge. Fuck! What the fuck is the point of this window being so damn big then? I want to pound my fists against it, but that would be stupid. He'd hear. I have to be quiet. I have to figure out something else.

I tiptoe to the door. My heart's trying to leap up my throat, but I keep moving. I have to try. I push my ear to the door and I can hear his voice, but I can't make out the words. He must be downstairs. I twist the knob, but it doesn't budge. I try again with both hands and it doesn't give. I look at the knob and see it's not locked, but then my eyes travel up. There's a second lock. Motherfucker!

I want to scream at that asshole. He locked me in! I'm locked in here like a bird in its gilded cage. I huff in a staggered breath and walk backwards slowly until I'm against the wall. I lower myself to the floor. I have to wait. I raise my head and cast a glance around the room. I need to find a weapon. I'm quick to get up with this thought in mind.

I may not be able to run, but I'll fight. I'll do whatever I have to. I pull open the drawer of the nightstand. It's empty except for a stack of papers. I go through his dresser, one drawer at a time. Nothing. Not a damn thing. I stare at the gun safe in the corner of the room. I can't imagine he left it unlocked, but I have to try anyway. I pull the door, but it's no use.

The bathroom. I race to the en suite, but keep my steps light. There has to be something in here. My eyes catch sight of a razor. It's not much, but it'll have to do. I grab the plastic handle and tilt it on its side on the counter. I need to crack the plastic so I can get to the blade.

My eyes search for anything that's hard and heavy enough to do the job. I finally see the tumbler by the sink. The bottom is stainless steel. I grab the towel from the hook and lay it on the counter to absorb some of the noise. I smash the tumbler on top of the razor, hard, but not hard enough to make much noise.

My heart stills and my blood rushes faster, waiting to hear anything from downstairs. Nothing. So I hit it again and again until the plastic cracks. I try pulling the plastic back, but I need more give. I tilt the razor and try to angle it so it'll be more effective. I raise my arm up and smash it down.

Yes! The plastic cracks even more, and I'm able to wiggle the blade out carefully. I raise the blade up to my eyes to look at the shiny, metal weapon. It's small. Really fucking small. But maybe if I can catch him by surprise, I'll be able to hurt him enough to escape.

"Whatcha doing, sweetheart?" I jump at the sound of Vince's voice and nearly drop the blade.

I stare at Vince from across the room. He sneaked up on me. How long has he been watching me? I don't answer him. Instead I make a fist and position the blade in the space between two of my fingers so it'll cut him when I swing.

We both know what I'm doing. My blood heats and rushes in my ears. My heart feels like it's trying to escape my body. It's beating that wildly. But I ignore my heart and blood both. Vince's gaze is hard and focused on me.

"You planning on hitting me, sweetheart?" He takes a step toward me and as much as I want to stand my ground, I instinctively take a step back. "You wanna hurt me, Elle?"

No. I don't. I don't want to hurt him.

"You wanna kill me baby, is that it?" I shake my head, but keep my eyes trained on him. I take another step back as he steps even closer. My back hits the wall. I'm cornered. Sweat covers my body with a chill.

"That's not very nice. Here I am trying to help you." He lunges for me and I try to hit him, but he grabs my wrist and forces my hand above my head. I scream and try to push him away as he twists my wrist and the blade slips through my fingers. Faintly, I hear the thin metal hit the tiled floor.

My body sags as he pushes his hard chest against me. I close my eyes and push my head against the wall. Sadness weakens my body.

He grips my jaw and forces me to face him, but I keep my eyes closed. I can't look at him. "You were going to kill me, sweetheart? You wanted to kill me?"

I try to shake my head but I can't. I try to speak, but with his hand on my jaw, I can't.

"Look at me!" he yells into my face, and it forces a whimper out of me, but my eyes stay closed.

Without any warning, he leaves me. My body falls limp to the floor and my knee slams down against the tile. Fuck! I grab it and lay on my side as the pain shoots up my body.

"Fuck, Elle!" He bends down beside me and picks me up off the floor. I expect his anger, not for him to take me gently into his arms. I bury my head in his chest. I can't take this. I'm not a person who can handle this kind of situation. I'm just breaking down. He walks me back over to the bed and sits down with me limp in his lap.

His hands pry my grip from my knee, and I watch his face as he looks it over, examining my injury. It'll bruise, but I'll be okay. It hardly hurts anymore. He's looking at me like I got shot. The concern on his face just doesn't make sense. He runs his fingers over the mark that will be a bruise. And then his dark eyes find mine. "You shouldn't have done that, sweetheart." There's a trace of a threat in his voice.

But there's something else, much stronger. Something that makes my breathing pick up. My fingers itch to run along the prick of his stubble. I want to grab his hair and push his lips to mine. Maybe I just want comfort, maybe it's something else. I don't know, but I want him. I *need* him.

I may die any minute now. I'm not going to hold back. I reach up and grip his hair, pulling myself to him and crushing my lips against his. His lips are hard at first and he pulls back, looking shocked, but also guarded.

"Please," I whisper. He answers by pushing my body against the mattress, keeping his lips on mine.

He pulls back and takes a shallow breath before asking me, "You think you can manipulate me with your pussy?" I shake my head. That's not it. That's not why.

"It's not going to work, sweetheart." He tries to pull away from me. And I can't stand the distance. I need this. I need to feel his hard body against me.

"Please," I beg again. If he denies me I don't know what I'll do. I feel sick with myself. But I won't refuse this need. I have for so long. Not again. I can't.

His hard body cages me in, and I find myself wanting more. Wanting to push him harder. His eyes spark with an unvoiced threat, but more than that--desire.

Yes!

"Please," I say again, and pull his lips to mine. His tongue dives into my mouth. I suck his bottom lip. His hips spread my legs and I part for him. I still hurt, but I need this. I need to get lost in his touch. I need to feel something other than this hopelessness and despair. His hands move to my thighs and push the hem of my dress up to my waist. I moan into his mouth as his erection pushes against my clit.

He breaks our kiss to look down at me. I'm panting beneath him, my fingers digging into the mattress. He pulls his shirt above his head, his muscles rippling with the movement.

"Take it off." I immediately obey him and pull at my straps and shove the dress off my body. I watch as he kicks his pants off and takes his hard dick in his hand to stroke it. He's the epitome of lust and power as he pushes my knees farther apart and runs his fingers down the thin fabric against my pussy, before pulling the panties down my thighs. I shudder under his touch. My body feels cold without his warmth. I need him.

"On your knees." I turn over and hate it. I don't want him to take me from behind like this. I feel him run the head of his cock from my entrance to my clit. The velvety feel of his head on my throbbing clit makes my back arch and I moan into the air. I want him to hold me while he fucks me. I want to feel like there's more than just lust, but before I can say anything he slams into me.

Fuck! I clench at the sheets, grasping handfuls of the fabric as I scream into the mattress. Holy fuck. That's intense. More than earlier. Much more. My legs tremble as he stills deep inside me. I'm so close to the edge of pain. The mix is a dark delicacy. I don't know how to handle it. I want to move away, the feeling too intense, too much. At the same time, I want to push back. I need more.

"Are you okay, Elle?" Vince whispers in my ear, and it's only then that I realize tears have leaked down my cheeks. My head shakes back and forth on its own accord.

He quickly withdraws, causing a bit of pain, and leaves me feeling empty and raw. He pulls me into his chest. "I'm sorry, sweetheart." He kisses my hair. "I didn't realize you were hurting." I brush the tears away with the back of my hand and try to pull myself together. I'm such a fucking mess.

"Do you always get this sore?" he asks me, and I huff a humorless laugh.

"I wouldn't know." I manage to push the words out while I lean down to wipe my face with the sheets.

"What do you mean?" he asks.

"You were my first." I bite the words out and regret admitting it immediately. I'm met with silence, and I don't dare look up at him to see his reaction.

His hands grip my hips and flip me onto my back. I gasp in shock and then stare wide-eyed as his head dips to my heat and he sucks my clit into his mouth. My fingers spear into his hair and my head falls back against the mattress as my eyes close. I push him further into my heat and try to rock my pussy on his face. I feel needy. I *am* needy. And he gives it to me.

His hot, wet tongue laps at my pussy, nibbling and sucking along every sensitive part. My clit is throbbing and in need of his touch. My pussy clenches around nothing. Finally, he satisfies both at the same time, massaging my clit with his tongue while dipping his fingers into my pussy. His fingers curve and rub the sensitive bundle of nerves at the front wall.

I close my eyes and moan into the air above me. My thighs start to tingle and my toes go numb. My body stiffens and I know it's coming. I know he's going to shatter me into a million pieces. His head lifts between my thighs with his fingers still inside me.

My mouth opens to object, but before I can utter a single word, he pinches my clit and pushes his tongue into my pussy, fucking me with it. The forcefulness of his deft fingers on me pushes me over the edge. Waves of heat and pleasure crash through my body.

Wave after wave of heated pleasure rocks through me.

I barely register him pulling away from me only to cage my body in.

He leaves hot, open-mouthed kisses on my neck, down to my collarbone. His hot breath tickles my neck, causing my nipples to harden. My head turns to the side as my breathing settles. I feel the head of his cock push into me. He moves deeper and deeper, slowly stretching my walls. His thumb pushes against my clit, making my entire body heat as a radiating pleasure builds in the pit of my stomach, threatening to take over my body. My head thrashes as I absorb the intense waves of pleasure mixed with the hint of pain from his large girth.

He kisses and licks his way down to the pale peaks of my

breasts and sucks them into his mouth. He rocks in and out of me slowly as he keeps one hand massaging my clit, while the other hand roams over the rest of my body. The combination of his expert touch and practiced motions overwhelms my senses. I tremble beneath him feeling the slow build of pleasure rising higher and higher, threatening to consume me. Fear paralyzes me. I don't know if I can handle this. It feels too high, too intense.

And then all at once, he pushes deeper into me, all the way to the hilt. As he thrusts, he pinches my clit while biting down on my nipple hard enough to cause just the tiniest hint of pain. With his free hand he pinches my other nipple between his fingers, and I explode beneath him. Overwhelmed with heat, every nerve ending in my body lights aflame. My back arches and my body stiffens.

As my orgasm crashes through every limb, Vince pounds me harder and harder, pushing the edge of my release higher up. His hands grip my ass and angle me to his rough pubic hair brushing against my clit with every violent thrust. My fingers claw at the sheets as my mouth hangs open in a silent scream of pleasure.

His head dips to the crook of my neck, and he nips my earlobe as he growls, "Mine."

He thrusts harder and faster, pistoning into me, the gentleness completely gone as he owns my body. "Mine," he says louder in my ear. His hot breath mingles in the suffocating air between us. His lips crash against mine with a primal need and I meet his passion, pouring everything into our kiss. His hands move to my thighs and spread me even wider for him.

I moan from how deep he enters me, hitting the opening of my cervix with every thrust. He's so deep, almost too deep. I feel the need to pull away, but each time he leaves me I want more. Again and again he thrusts mercilessly into me.

I feel the rising tingling through my body. My breathing comes in heavy pants. My lungs seem too empty, not filling fast enough. The need to breathe barely registers as he forces himself deep inside of me and hot waves of cum splash inside me. I feel him pulse as his eyes go half-lidded and his mouth hangs open in ecstasy. The sight of him in complete pleasure and the feel of his cock pumping inside of me sets me off. I shatter beneath him yet again.

The heat, the tingling sensation along every inch of my skin is too much. I want to thrash and move against the overwhelming feelings, but instead I'm paralyzed. My body bows, and the heels of my feet dig into his ass. My pussy clamps hard around him and I scream his name as I cum violently around him.

As my breathing slows and my heart settles, the hot, numbing feeling on my skin begins to subside. But every small movement sends a jolt of pleasure through my body.

Vince moves me, picking my small body up in his arms and spooning beside me, my back pressed against his front.

He plants small kisses on my neck and runs his hand down my side, over my hip, ending at the top of my thigh. Once my breathing has calmed, he pulls the blanket over me and wraps his arm around my chest, molding my body to his and holding me tight.

It's everything I thought it would be like. I close my eyes and try to keep reality from coming back. I can't avoid it. The second I try to resist, it floods back to me and I stiffen in his arms.

He tries to soothe me, to mold my back to his chest, but I resist.

After a long while, Vince finally speaks. "I need to get out of here." He lets me go and moves off the bed.

I sit up to look at him. "Where..." I start to question him, but I stop. I'm fucking stupid for thinking there was something there between us. That I felt something for him. I close my mouth and try to gather up the courage to ask to leave again. I just want to go. The thought is like a brick in my stomach.

"I just want to leave. I'm not going to say anything about anything." I try to cross my legs on the bed, but fuck, I hurt so bad. I'm so sore. I wince slightly and a look of pain is reflected in Vince's eyes.

"You're not going anywhere, sweetheart. I need to figure this shit out."

"You're just making it worse!" I yell at him.

"You don't understand." His cool response makes me angry.

"Explain it to me then!"

He grips my mouth with one hand and grabs the nape of my neck with the other. He lowers his head and kisses me hard on the lips. "Sweetheart, I swear to God, you really need to shut your mouth and trust me."

I want to. I want to trust him, but I can't.

"I need to tie you up." No. I don't want that. I shake my head, no.

"Why?" I ask in a hoarse whisper.

He stares at me like I'm an idiot. "You just tried to kill me."

"You just fucked me," I spit back.

"It was a lapse in judgment." That fucking hurt. That's a damn blow to my ego. Shame replaces any possible positive feeling I have.

He must see the hurt on my face. "Not like that. I didn't mean it like that."

I can't look at him. He tries to touch me and I push him away.

It was a mistake. All of this is such a mistake. I'm a mistake. I've heard it all my life, but I never thought it was true until now. I don't want to die, but part of me wishes he would just kill me.

CHAPTER 21

VINCE

I don't fucking want to be here. I shouldn't be here. Instead, I should be making sure that she's staying put. But I tied her up so tight, there's no way she's getting out.

She was a virgin. She lost her virginity to me like that. No wonder she was so fucking sore. I tilt my head back and slam down another shot. So fucking tight. So fucking good.

I don't know what the fuck I'm doing. Billy lines up another shot for me. His eyes are full of pity. I'm sure everyone knows. Everyone's avoiding me. I'm guessing they think I killed her. The occasional pats on the back and squeezes of my shoulder as they walk by tell me that's what they're thinking.

They feel sorry for me that I'm so fucked up over having

to kill her. Or having killed her, depending on whether they think I went through with it already.

I take another shot. I'm so fucking drunk.

What was I thinking? Like I could just keep her, and that would solve the problem? She saw. They saw. She has to die. It's as simple as that. But I don't want that. And I always get what I want. It's not fucking happening. I won't let it happen.

"Did you take care of that issue?" Anthony asks looking at my mangled hand. Everyone keeps looking at it. I know what they're thinking. And I fucking hate it.

"Which issue?" I ask sarcastically. I know he's talking about Elle. But the fucking cartel is a pain in my ass, too.

I put the edge of another shot glass against my lips and shake my head before throwing it back. My body starts to tingle, and my teeth seem to go numb. Good. I want to be fucking wasted. My phone stopped going off in my pocket a little while ago. I take it that means someone told Pops that I'm here. I wonder what he thinks. Specifically, what he thinks of her. Not to mention what he thinks of me and my fucked up decisions.

"It's not like she's yours, Vince. It fucking sucks." Anthony puts a hand on his chest. "She was just in the wrong place, at the wrong time. I fucking hurt for her, I do." I can see it in his eyes that he doesn't like it, that he does have remorse. "But this is the entire family we're talking about." I nod my head solemnly. "If she talks, we're fucked." He takes a drink of his beer. "She's not one of us. She's not a *comare*. They'll make her talk. You know how they harass anyone who comes in here. If they saw her, they'll make her talk."

I take another swig and almost choke as the perfect solution hits me. I need to knock her up. I need to marry my sweetheart. They won't touch her if she's mine. No one will touch her if she's mine. And if I get my way, she's going to be mine. And the police can't make her testify against me if she's my wife. No one will be able to threaten her.

She. Is. Mine. I repress the need to scream it into everyone's face. I want them all to know. She's not going anywhere. I push away from the bar and slide off the stool. It wobbles, then tips over as my feet hit the ground. I walk forward and reach for my car keys in my pocket.

"Whoa, Vince. What the fuck, dude?" I hear Anthony pick up my stool, then come up behind me, grabbing at my elbow to make me stop.

"I gotta go," I say simply. I do. I need to get back to Elle. He walks in front of me to stop me in my path.

"You're trashed, man." I shrug my shoulders.

"She needs me, Anthony." I'm vaguely aware that the bar is quiet. I can feel their eyes on me. I know everyone in here. It's all familia. And they're all watching.

"Hey, calm down. Let's talk this out, Vince," he says. I shake my head and take a step closer to him.

"She's mine," I growl in his face. His hands come up in a

gesture of surrender.

"Alright. I get that. No one's taking her from you."

"Damn right no one's going to touch her!" I scream it as loud as I can. I feel like a fucking fool. It's not smart to yell. It's not wise to lose your cool. But I can't fucking help it. I want everyone to know she's mine. I run my fingers through my hair, then take a deep breath. "I'm gonna make her mine and no one's going to hurt Elle." I stare at him as I speak calmly, but everyone here knows I'm talking to them, too. From my periphery I can see my men nodding.

"No one's going to touch her," Anthony says, and I feel Tommy come up to my right side and lay a hand on my shoulder.

"You need a ride, boss?" he asks.

"Yeah, I need to get back to her, Tommy." My words slur a bit and I pinch the bridge of my nose as we walk towards the doors.

"You know, I feel bad for your girl, Vince," Anthony says from behind me loud enough for everyone to hear. I turn to face him. "She's gonna have to deal with your whiskey dick tonight."

I grin at him and laugh. After a split second, the rest of the bar joins in on the joke.

A calmness settles in my chest. For the first time since all this shit happened, I feel like it might be alright.

I may get to keep my sweetheart after all. I just need to knock her up first.

CHAPTER 22

VINCE

I don't remember why I'm so fucking horny for her. But I am. It takes me at least four tries to get the key in the lock to the door. But I fucking did it and I feel like a champion for getting into the house. Rigs is barking and barreling down the stairs like a good boy. I bet he was laying outside her room. I feel like an asshole as I watch him squatting in the yard. I gotta get up there and make sure she's still alright. I close the door after he gets his furry butt inside and we make our way up the stairs. I leave him out in the hall and ignore his little whine when I don't let him in. I gotta get him a giant ass bone for dealing with this shit. I huff up a laugh as I walk, I'm fairly certain, straight to the bed. Right where I left my sweetheart all tied up.

Her wrists are bound with a silk tie and it's wrapped around a rod on the headboard. It doesn't look very comfortable, but she appears to be sleeping. I grip my shirt and pull it over my head, then shove my pants down. I palm my raging erection and stroke it up and down while my eyes travel over her body. She's in one of my tees. It's bunched around her hips and there's a nice red mark still on her thigh from where I was gripping her earlier. I groan and stroke my dick again before climbing on the bed.

Mine. All mine.

The creak of my movements and the dip of the bed gets her attention and she stares back at me with her lips parted. I take it she's surprised to see me. Her legs scissor as she tries to turn and lift herself up. But with her wrists bound she can hardly move. My dick bobs up and down as I crawl across the bed. I grab her ass with both hands and push her up higher so she can sit how she'd like.

Feeling her bare ass in my hands only makes me want her more. I remember that she's not wearing any panties. My cock gets even harder.

I feel lightheaded and groggy as I crawl closer to her.

"I got it figured out, Elle." I move her ass up higher on the bed again so there's less pressure on her arms.

"Vince?" she asks in a tired voice. She looks a little out of it. I know she's gotta be tired.

"Yeah, baby?" I rub her shoulders to help ease the tension.

"It really hurt me, what you said before you left." I love how straight forward she is. I kiss her shoulder to reward her.

"I wish I could take it back. I wish I could take it all back. You don't deserve this."

She looks at me with those big blue eyes and pleads for an answer. "What are you going to do to me?"

I finally have an answer for her. I smirk at her, "I'm going to keep you."

Her eyes widen and her lips part. "I'm gonna make you mine." I kiss down her body and settle between her legs. A small pant comes from that gorgeous mouth of hers and her thighs clench. I don't know if she loves the idea, but she sure as fuck seems turned on by it.

"Spread your legs for me, sweetheart." I'm sure some of those words are slurred, but she obeys. I drop to my elbows and push her thighs further apart. I run a finger from her sensitive clit, which makes her body shiver, all the way down to the entrance of her pussy. She's hot.

And red.

Too red. My poor girl's gotta be sore. I wanted to be gentle with her earlier. But knowing I had this virgin pussy all to myself broke a wall inside me and let out a beast that I didn't know I had in me.

I push my thumb against her throbbing clit and grin as her back bows and her arms pull against the restraints. She's still primed for yet another orgasm. What a greedy little pussy. I lower my head and push her legs apart further with my shoulders, then take a languid lick of her heat. I wiped her off after I tied her up, but I can still taste some of our combined cum on her pussy. I don't give a fuck. My tongue dips into her pussy. I keep my movements easy and gentle. She's too sore. I just want to soothe her.

My dick jumps in disagreement. Maybe not. That's right--I need to knock her up. That'll keep everyone away from her. I groan into her heat and suck her clit into my mouth. My sweetheart tries to ride my face and I fucking love it. She's not afraid to ask for what she wants. She just goes for it. I suck her clit hard and push a finger into her to rub her G-spot and push her over the edge. She's too fucking easy to get off. She's so damn tight I feel her clamp down on my finger as her orgasm takes over. I let her clit go with a pop and lick my lips.

So fucking sweet.

I crawl over her trembling body and reach up to untie her wrists. I want her on top, riding me. I want to watch her tits bounce as she fucks herself on my dick.

And then I remember.

It's a shock to my system remembering how she tried to run from me. How she wanted to get away. Just hours ago she was going to fight me to try to leave. I can't blame her, but fuck me if it doesn't hurt. I look at her face, eyes closed in rapture as she bites down on her bottom lip. Right now she's being my sweetheart. But I can't untie her. What if she up and runs? Fuck! I can't let that shit happen. I can't be sloppy.

Tomorrow she's going to learn she belongs to me now. Neither of us has a choice. I flop down on the bed beside her and pull her ass against my dick. I take a deep breath in the crook of her neck, loving the way she smells. My eyes feel heavy and my body sags deeper into the warmth of the bed. I haphazardly grab the comforter and pull it over our bodies.

Tomorrow. I hug her body close to mine and splay my hand over her belly.

I'm going to make her mine tomorrow.

CHAPTER 23

ELLE

I wake up to the bright light coming in from the window. It hurts my eyes, but I can't block it. My arms won't move over my face. Vince's heavy and so hot, laying against my body. His chest is molded to my back and his arms are wrapped tight around me. His weight puts more pressure on my arms. Fuck it hurts. His scent fills my lungs, a woodsy pine and masculine smell, mixed with the faint odor of whiskey. I moan softly, loving how he smells. And then I get angry from my reaction.

I hate that I want him. He stirs behind me, and I hold my breath. I feel his grin on my neck. "Elle, sweetheart, you keep fucking me up, you know that?" His words are slurred and full of sleep.

"Vince?" I ask in a voice loud enough for him to hear, but

not so loud that it would wake him.

"I'm gonna put a baby in you. Then they won't hurt you, sweetheart." He whispers his words against the side of my neck. *A baby.* "No one's gonna lay a finger on my girl." He pulls my back up against his chest again and rocks his dick against my ass.

"Vince?" I ask again, a little louder. I get no response.

Holy fuck. He wants to knock me up? That's his plan? I can't help the fact that the very thought of being pregnant with his child makes me want him inside me.

I feel alive in his arms. I want to get lost in his touch.

But a baby? It's life-changing.

Once I'm pregnant though, I'm sure he won't hurt me. Hope lights inside of me. I can have his baby. If that's the cost, I'll pay the price. I'll be a good mother. I've always wanted a child, but never thought it would happen. Maybe this is a blessing. Everything happens for a reason.

I calm my racing heart. Maybe I don't even need to really get pregnant. I can just go along with the plan.

His phone goes off from somewhere in the room and interrupts my thoughts. My body stiffens as Vince turns away from me and groans.

He rolls to the edge of the bed and presses his palms to his eyes. His broad, muscular back ripples with his movements as he stretches and reaches down to pick up his jeans to retrieve his phone.

"Hey Pops," he answers only a little drowsily and then yawns, holding the phone away from his ear.

"What's going on, Vince? I'm worried over here." Ever so faintly, I can hear his father's voice.

"Everything's good," Vince speaks into the phone, and then looks back over his shoulder at me. He moves quickly to my side and starts untying the knot on my wrists with one hand. *Thank fuck!* My shoulders are killing me.

"You still got her?" his father asks.

"Yeah." Vince props the phone between his ear and shoulder so he can use both hands while he's untying me. "It's all good." Hearing him say that makes my heart swell with hope. But I know why he's saying that. I know what he's planning, and that makes my heart harden.

"Good. I'm coming over." Vince stills for a moment and then pulls the tie away. My shoulders sag as I'm released, and I wince with pain as I move my arms down to my side.

Vince is quiet, but then he answers his father, "Alright Pops. You bringing breakfast?" He answers lightheartedly, but the look on his face doesn't match his tone.

CHAPTER 24

ELLE

"That feel any better?" Vince asks, as he sets the heating pad on my shoulders. Once he was off the phone with his father, he spent a good 20 minutes rubbing feeling back into my arms and quietly apologizing. The heat and his touch feel so good. My shoulders and arms are still sore, but I give him a small smile and nod. I lean back in his dining room chair and bring my cup of coffee to my lips. He hasn't said much this morning, and neither have I. Things have changed. Drastically.

I remember what he said in his sleep, and while part of me is terrified of him really wanting to knock me up, the other part is worried he's changed his mind. Or that it was just a dream. That he doesn't want to be tied to me, and it'll be easier to just kill me. So I've behaved. I've listened to everything. I'll do whatever I have to in order to survive.

"We need to have a talk, Elle." He rounds the grey granite countertop and walks into the kitchen. The open concept design of the space gives a light and airy feel, but I'm practically suffocating from nerves.

"I'm listening," I say, and take another sip of coffee. My eyes stay on him so he knows he has my attention. He's wearing those pajama pants slung low on his hips again. He gave me an identical pair to wear, but I'm drowning in them.

"I need for you to be patient with me." He looks out of the window and shoves his hands in his pockets. "I believe you, sweetheart, but they won't. Even if they do, they won't risk it."

"Won't risk what?" I ask.

"Rule one." He holds up a finger and walks back over to the dining room to take a seat at the chair next to me. He leans forward in his seat as he looks at me intently. "Don't ask questions."

I open my mouth to ask why, but then I close it and purse my lips. An asymmetric grin grows on his face. "Learning already."

"No questions. Understood." I really don't like that. I like to ask questions so I can know things. But then again, I already know too much.

"What do you remember, baby?" he asks.

I take a deep breath and set the mug down on the dark maple tabletop. "I remember--"

He cuts me off. "Nothing. Rule two, you don't remember a damn thing, and you don't know what anyone is talking about." My eyes dart to his. His face is all hard lines and seriousness.

I pick up my mug and take a sip. "I don't remember a damn thing."

"That's right--you don't." He leans down and picks my feet up to put on his lap. His thumbs dig into the soles as he massages my feet. I moan into the cup. It feels so good. "I'm going to take care of you until things settle down. Everything is going to be fine, alright?"

I meet his soft gaze and nod. "Mmm hmm."

He gives me a tight smile. "That brings us to rule number three." He keeps rubbing my feet and holds my gaze. "Who do you belong to, Elle?"

I feel my eyes widen and my heart skips a beat. I know the answer, but it's caught in my throat. I swallow the lump in my throat and answer him with a whisper. "You."

"That's right. And you're going to listen to what I say, aren't you, sweetheart? You're going to do as you're told."

My pussy clenches at his words. He obviously doesn't realize how fucking hot that makes me. I'm fucked up in the head for wanting him like that in this very moment, but I do. I nod my head to try to keep the lust from coming through my voice.

"Answer me, sweetheart." There's an admonishment in his tone and he stops rubbing my feet.

"Yes. I'll do as I'm told." My voice comes out breathy and

a smirk kicks up his lips. He drops my feet to the floor and moves closer to me, but a hard knock at the door interrupts us.

He stands up, then bends at the waist to cup my jaw and plant a kiss on my lips. It's forceful and full of need. "Stay here, sweetheart."

My heart races in my chest. I've agreed to be his, and I fucking love that idea. But I have no idea if it'll be enough to save me.

I hear Vince open the door and I grip the mug with both of my hands. Surely anyone in my position would say they'd listen. They'd do whatever they could to stay alive. I just hope he believes me. Because it's true. I'll listen to him. I *want* to listen to him. Some sick part of me wants to be his.

Heavy footsteps bring my eyes up past the kitchen to the foyer. His father has an arm braced around Vince's shoulders and he's talking in his ear. I don't like it. It makes me feel uneasy, like he's trying to convince Vince to get rid of me.

Vince must feel my eyes on him, because he looks over in my direction and stares back at me. He smiles at me and turns to his father. His warm expression relaxes me some. My shoulders feel heavy with weight of the heating pad so I pull it off and stand on shaky legs.

"No need to stand for me, Elle." Vince's father gives me a tight smile. His hair is peppered with grey and his eyes are a light blue. The laugh lines on his face make his age apparent, but his body is still muscular. There's no doubt in my mind that he's lethal.

I swallow thickly and try to smile up at him, but I can't. My mind keeps racing with the memory of yesterday. My hands grip the back of the chair.

"Sweetheart, go grab yourself another cup of coffee." Vince places his hand on the small of my back. My eyes are focused on the table as I try to will my fingers to just let go. I nod and as soon as I release the chair, I grab my cup and walk quickly to the kitchen. I stand with my back to them trying to listen to their whispers. I can't make out what they are saying.

Tears come to my eyes and my heart races. This is stupid, so fucking stupid. He isn't going to keep me. They're going to kill me. I walk to the sink and dump the lukewarm remains of my coffee down the drain. My hands grip the front of the sink, and it feels like my legs are going to collapse. I close my eyes and try to steady my breathing. My back is still to them.

If they're going to kill me, I wish they'd do it like this. During some mundane activity like washing the dishes or something. That'd be an okay way to go, I guess, if I didn't see it coming. I squeeze my eyes shut and then jump and scream at the feel of hands on my waist.

"Sweetheart." There's a note of warning in Vince's tone. "Whatever's going on in your head, knock it off."

I force my eyes open, but I can't turn to face him. "If you're going to kill me, please do it when I don't see it coming."

"Elle, stop it." Vince pulls my body close to his so that my back is right up against his chest. He kisses my neck. I don't know if he knows how comforting and at ease it makes me for him to hold me like this right now, especially in front of his father. It makes his claim to me that much more real.

"No one's going to hurt you." I hear Vince's father and a sense of calm moves through my body. I dare to take a look at Vince's father. "I promise you, we have no intentions of hurting you."

"I told you you're mine, didn't I?" Vince asks me. I nod my head against Vince's shoulder and try to stop my nerves from getting the better of me.

"No one touches what's mine."

CHAPTER 25

VINCE

"**Y**ou wanna pick some stuff out or something?" I push the laptop to Elle across the table. Pops left after having a private conversation with me about the shipments. I have a small list of names I need to handle to get shit back on the up and up on that front. They've got to know it's coming though, since Javier made sure to take care of his end as soon as he found out who was stealing from him. Their partners getting murdered is a good sign that we're coming for them. The Locos Diablos MC is gonna be short a few members real fucking soon. They're an offshoot of Shadows MC, essentially their rejects. They're fucking stupid to think they'd start a war between the *familia* and the cartel by stealing from us.

And then there's the issue of Elle's mother, Sandra Hawthorne. She's got to be dealt with, but I don't feel like handling that issue right now.

"You're letting me go online? What if I emailed someone?" she asks with disbelief. Leave it to her to give me a reason that I shouldn't let her go online. She's questioning everything she's doing, which is good, but I want her to get comfortable. I want her to just act natural, like how she was when I took her for the first time. That moment in time is what I want every day.

"Don't. I'm going to be right here. Just pick out what you need." She reaches for the laptop and slowly opens it.

"I could just get some things from my house," she offers.

"Your mother already tried reporting you missing. You can't leave." I'm short with her, but it's for a good reason. All she has to do is listen to what I tell her and everything will be fine.

"What?" she asks, looking at me with her eyes opened wide.

"Rule one, sweetheart." She opens and then closes her mouth. I can tell she's going to have a hard time with that one. It can't hurt to let her know what's going on with her mother though. I'm gonna have her give her mother a call sometime soon, but right now it's too soon. "We have a guy on the inside, a police officer. Luckily he's the one that got the call."

"I'm surprised my mom gave a shit." Her voice turns sad and her eyes focus back on the laptop. I don't like it.

Apparently someone saw Elle with me and went to her mom's place to try and question her about me. Sandra didn't say shit to the police, which is good. It means my sweetheart really didn't remember anything that happened at the bistro until she came to my parents' house yesterday. It didn't piss me off that Sandra tried to file a missing person's report. But the fact that she attempted to make a will for my sweetheart today really fucking pisses me off.

"I don't understand why you put up with that shit." I'm not going to keep my mouth shut anymore. If she's going to be mine, her mother's going to have to back off and get her shit straightened out. I can tell this is going to be a fight, but I don't want it to be one.

"And what'd she do that got you so pissed off, huh? I mean on the night I met you. You were all bent out of shape." Elle doesn't have to tell me though, because I already know what she did. I got the report from Tony. It has everything on my girl. And there's a ton of shit there. A ton of debt, to be specific. I know her mother took it out, too. She tried to file for loans a few times with just Elle's name on the paperwork. Fucking bitch. I had to call Dom to have his guys transfer money from my account to Elle's and wipe her debt. I know Sandra's gonna do it again soon. As soon as she realizes she can. And I'm not looking forward to having to shut that shit down. I'll throw her thieving ass in jail. That's what she fucking deserves.

"She's my mother." I shake my head and bite my tongue. I know all about family. For fuck's sake, I have the entire *familia* to worry about.

"You're a strong woman. I hate to see you being taken advantage of." It's true, but she gives me a disbelieving look and I swear she almost rolls her eyes. I'm glad she's finally getting over that shit from earlier today, but my little sweetheart isn't gonna walk all over me.

"Don't look at me like that." I lower my voice to a threatening level, but she ignores it.

"You don't want to see me taken advantage of?" she asks without any sarcasm in her tone, but I know it's there.

"What the hell am I supposed to do, Elle?" I ask her, but I don't know why. I should really end this conversation. We shouldn't be talking about this shit.

"Just let me go." It fucking hurts that she's asking that. Even if I could, I wouldn't.

"They'll know. Then we're both dead." My blood freezes. If I fuck this up and she talks, I probably am dead. The family can't risk weakness like that.

"We can run," she whispers.

"We?" She wants to run away with me? It fills my chest with hope for us. But I'm not fucking running. I love this life. She'll learn to love it, too.

Her eyes fall and she focuses them on the screen.

"Answer me. You wanna go away with me?" I ask.

"I don't know. I don't have anyone else." I want her to want me, plain and simple. But not because she has no one else. That means someone could get between us and I don't like that.

"Get over here, sweetheart." I push my chair out and pat my thigh. She obeys immediately, walking quickly to me and sitting down on my lap.

"You would run away with me?" I wrap my arms around her waist.

"Yeah, I would. Does that make me stupid?" she asks.

"I care about you, Elle. Do you believe that?" My heart sputters in my chest. She better believe it. Because it's true. I don't know how or why, but I do care about her. I want her to be happy with me.

"I do." I love those words on her lips. I groan as my dick hardens and I rock it into her ass. I'm gonna hear those words again. Real fucking soon.

CHAPTER 26

VINCE

Fuck, today was a hassle. I can't find those MC pricks. They're in hiding now that they know we're gunning for them. And I know they'll be gunning for us, too. At least the shipments came in right this time. I toss my keys down on the table and bend down to let Rigs to lick my face.

"Good boy." I pet behind his ears for a minute. But my eyes are focused on the stairs. It feels good to have my sweetheart in my house. Not the safe house, but *my* house. Even though she's making it look more like *our* house with all the shit she has.

It's been two weeks. Two weeks of filling her greedy, needy cunt with my seed and trying to knock her up. The guys know we're together. They've backed off entirely on the issue of her being a witness. Now they wanna meet her, get to know my girl. I'm just waiting for the right time. I want her ready. I want her to know without a doubt she belongs to me.

She called her mom like I told her to. Did everything the *familia* wanted and asked of her to make them comfortable with her being mine. There's nothing standing between us now.

I smirk as I walk up the stairs. Rigs follows me and I let him, but I put my foot in front of him to stop him from coming into the room. he's used to it now.

I shut the door and turn to face my sweetheart. She's tied up on the bed. She tells me she hates it, that I can trust her and don't have to tie her up when I leave. But that pussy of hers is always soaked when I get home. Her pussy knows it belongs to me. She's ready for me every day. I know it's 'cause she's tied up. She says she hates it, but I know she's lying. She fucking loves it.

She's gagged for being a naughty girl this morning. Her panties are in her mouth for talking back to me. I need to get more ties. I've got one around her wrists, one keeping her panties in her mouth, and two more around her ankles, keeping her spread open for me. I went all out this morning since I knew I wouldn't be long. I wasn't gone for even an hour. And every minute was fucking torture for me. I kick my pants off and walk closer to the bed.

I stare at her pussy that's just waiting for me. It's glistening with her juices and my dick jumps in my pants with a desperate need to be inside her.

My eyes lock on hers. "Did you learn your lesson, sweetheart?" She nods her head obediently. She's fucking perfect. She's my obedient sweetheart. All fucking mine.

"I'm not sure you did." I shove two fingers into her tight pussy and pump them in and out. She pulls against the restraints, but her ass isn't going anywhere. Her moan is muffled by the panties in her mouth. I pull my fingers out before she can cum and remove the tie from around her mouth. She spits out her panties and pants. Her eyes are on me, just waiting to hear what I have to tell her. So fucking perfect.

I smack a hand down on her pussy. Slap! Her head falls back, and she moans again with pleasure. It's music to my ears. She's so fucking close already. I love keeping her on the edge. "Now, whose pussy is this?"

"Your pussy," she's quick to answer, and I reward her by pushing down on her clit and rubbing small circles. She struggles against the pleasure.

"Damn right it's my pussy." I push against her front wall with my fingers and smile as her walls tighten and her cum soaks my hand. She's been waiting for a full hour to cum. I should give her another.

I pull the ties free from around her ankles, but keep her wrists bound. My hips keep her legs open as I line my cock up. I lean down and kiss my sweetheart and she kisses me back with passion. I slam into her all the way to the hilt and fuck her mercilessly. She pulls her lips away to scream out my name.

That's right. My name. This pussy is mine. She's mine, all fucking mine. I pick up her legs and place her calves on my shoulders. Her eyes go wide as I slam in deeper and deeper, taking her to a new edge of pain and pleasure. Her pussy is so fucking tight like this. She's squeezing the hell out of my dick.

"Vince!" she yells out, as her legs start to tremble. Fuck yeah. Keep screaming my name.

My balls draw up watching her chest rise and fall, and her eyes nearly roll back in her head. My spine tingles as I push my dick as deep into her as I can. I cum violently as the head of my dick butts up against her cervix. A shudder goes through my body as her pussy spasms just as violently, matching the intensity of my orgasm, and she cries out in pleasure.

My lips crush against hers, silencing her moans and I reach one hand up to untie her wrists. It doesn't take long. I've had plenty of practice.

Her hands grip and tug my hair and she kisses me harder. She fucking loves me. I know she does. I wrap my arms around her body and roll her onto my chest. She pulls back with her eyes closed, lips slightly swollen from our bruising kiss. Her hair's a mess, looking just-fucked and her skin is flushed. The sight of her in complete rapture makes my heart swell.

All that shit was worth it.

"You got some boxes, baby," I call out over my shoulder as I pick up a box. She's been getting a shit-ton of packages. Books, makeup, clothes, art supplies, all sorts of shit. It makes me happy that she's finally feeling more comfortable with me buying her things. Not to mention that now she's got her painting hobby to have something to focus on.

I look suspiciously at the box in my hands and then at the remainder of the packages on the porch. They aren't marked or labeled in any way. I don't fucking like it. At first I assumed they were something she ordered, but there's no indication that these were sent through the mail. Someone left them here. I hear her coming down the stairs and I hold an arm out to stop her from coming any closer. I don't know what's in the boxes, but she's not going to be around when I open them.

"Elle, don't--" She pushes past me and screams out.

"Fucking bitch!" Elle cuts me off, and I turn to her in shock. That kind of language doesn't come out of my sweetheart's mouth. Her eyes are glassy with tears, but her facial expression reads that she's pissed.

"They're mine. I didn't get a chance to unpack them. My mother must've brought them over." I can feel her anger brewing. All over her mother. Sandra. What'd she do now?

"What'd she send you?" I can only guess that whatever's in the box, it's not wanted or needed, based on how Elle kicks the box and storms away. I debate on taking the boxes inside, but I'll wait till I find out what they contain.

"Sweetheart, answer me," I call out for her across the hall. She falls into the sofa looking defeated. Sandra really pisses me off. The only time my sweetheart is unhappy is when she hears from her mother.

"They're my boxes of things that were at her house. At *my* house. I didn't even get to unpack them." She pauses and then continues. "I told her she could come for a visit." She presses her lips together and crosses her arms over her knees, pulling them into her chest. She's a mix of hurt and anger and I'm not sure which is going to win out.

"Okay?" I don't understand. I must be missing something.

"I told her I couldn't give her any money since I wasn't working, but she could come see me if she wanted." I know all of this already. She asked me what I thought about that arrangement beforehand, and I agreed that would be wise. Elle's a smart girl. Plus, she enjoys this arrangement as much as I do. She hasn't done a damn thing suspicious and asks for permission before doing anything. I get the feeling she really enjoys me having the control in our relationship, which I fucking love.

"I'm missing something," I say. The tears in her eyes fall down her cheeks and she wipes them away angrily.

"I didn't tell you what she said," she answers.

"She said I was a selfish bitch for abandoning her, and that I could come get my shit."

I keep my voice light and don't let it show how pissed I am. I have to work real fucking hard to keep my anger out of my expression. I've never wished ill on a woman before, but I can't stand that bitch, Elle's mother or not. "Well at least she saved you the trip." Elle rolls her eyes and doesn't even crack a smile. I know it hurts her. If she could, she'd give her mom everything and I know her mother would take it all, too. Now that Elle's mine, it's not happening.

I have to do something to make her smile. I don't like her being so upset. "Do you have a nice dress to wear, sweetheart?" She looks back at me, tilting her head with a questioning look on her face. I raise my brows, waiting for an answer.

She shakes her head slowly. "Only my sundress." She hasn't been out of this house in two weeks. She's got to want to get out of here. I'm surprised with all the shit she's bought lately that she hasn't ordered another dress.

"Well, go put it on--I wanna take you out tonight." Her eyes brighten and a wide smile grows on her face. She hops up and runs to me to wrap her arms around my back, planting a small kiss on my lips.

"How much time do I have?" she asks, all peppy like. I've been afraid to take her out. A small part of me questions her loyalty to me, as though this has all just been an act. Like she's just waiting to get away from me. A deep pain shoots through my chest at these thoughts, but I ignore it.

"Take as much time as you need, sweetheart. We can go wherever you'd like." I'll spoil her to the point that the thought of leaving me doesn't exist for her. If she leaves me, I don't know what would happen.

The guys have been hounding me to bring her around. They all wanna meet her. I know what they must think. I'm sure they can't believe she really *wants* to be with me.   Part of me doesn't believe it either. That doubt creeps up on me while I'm away from her.

But every time I get home and find her waiting for me, that doubt vanishes.   When she yammers on about some recipe on the cooking shows she watches, there's no doubt in my fucking mind that she wants to be with me. Either that, or she's trying to kill me with domestication.

It's time the guys met her. We'll all go out. They'll see her, and she'll see them. It's gotta happen at some point. A part of me wants to keep her here with all this tension between the MCs and the *familia*, but it'll be alright. We haven't gotten those fuckers yet and Javier's breathing fire down our necks, but I can't keep her locked in here forever. She needs to get out and have some fun.

"Let's get out of the house, baby. I wanna show you off."

CHAPTER 27

ELLE

My nerves are shot. My palms are sweaty, and I can hardly breathe. I'm going to meet the *familia*. The Don is Dante, Vince's father. I don't know much about anyone else, though. Well, except that Dom and Tommy were the two that I ... met already. I breathe in deep and shake out my hands as we stand in front of the restaurant doors.

"They're going to love you." I hear Vince's voice and my heart hammers in my chest. I just don't believe it. I swallow thickly. They want me dead I'm sure. It'd be stupid for me to think otherwise. I see my reflection in the mirror and I cringe. I can't get this stupid panicked look off my face.

I turn to face Vince and try to bail. "I changed my mind."

"Stop it, Elle." He opens the door and puts his hand on the small of my back. "Just be yourself." I take a deep breath and try not to freak out. Everything's going to be fine. Vince won't let anyone hurt me. That thought soothes me. Every part of me calms, because it's true. He won't let anyone touch me. *I'm his.*

I look around the table, and the only people I know are the three I met. The two men, Dom and Tommy, I haven't seen since the incident. It chills me to the core to set eyes on them. But when Dom sees me, he stands and smiles. "Vince, I'm happy you finally brought her out!" Dom walks to me with quick strides and kisses my cheek. Vince loosens his grip on me and leaves my side to give his mother a kiss on the cheek. Without him beside me I feel vulnerable.

The last two weeks have been the same every day. And I'm almost ashamed to say I've enjoyed it. I don't fear Vince at all. I know he wants me. In his eyes, I belong to him, and he takes care of me in a way I desire. It's a sick fantasy come to life. Well, some of it. Our days are almost normal until he has to leave for work. Every morning we wake up beside each other, exchange small talk, and drink coffee. We joke around like a normal couple, banter like a normal couple. It's almost easy to forget that we're anything but normal.

When he leaves is when everything changes. Or at night, before we go to bed. I like to pretend it's a fantasy, a game we like to play. It makes it that much sweeter. I don't want it to stop. I know that's bad. I'm sure it's not healthy. But I fucking love when he ties me up. I know he's going to reward me and fuck me like he owns my body. Just thinking about it turns me on. But it's wrong. It's so wrong.

I haven't left his house in two full weeks. I've barely spoken to anyone but Vince and my mother. Vince wanted me to call her since she filed a missing person's report. It fucking killed me to think she was worried, but when she answered the phone she seemed more pissed than anything. I almost asked Vince to let me go see her. Almost. But I'd rather stay inside the house with him. It's all so wrong. But it feels so good. I don't worry about anything. I enjoy being his. I'm sure a shrink would tell me I'm insane. And maybe I am.

Being here in this restaurant with these people emphasizes how fucked up this situation is. He's told me about each of them. His brother Dom, and Dom's wife Becca are on the right side of the table. I know Dom's a professor and that Becca owns this restaurant. His father is seated at the head of the table on the far end, and Vince's mother is seated next to Becca. His cousin Joey's here. I know he has a son, but I don't see him here. An older man is sitting next to him, that must be Uncle Enzo. And then there's Tommy and Anthony, Vince's cousins, sitting together on the left side of the table. Looking at the two of them reminds me of my memory. Of them looking at me like I'm a threat. I still don't know what I did or what I saw. I just remember Vince pinning me down and them staring at me like I had to die. My palms grow sweaty and I wipe them on the sides of my dress.

"You want a drink, Elle?" Tommy asks me from across the room. He gives me a smile as he takes a sip of his wine.

"Please," I respond as normally as I can, given the situation and my nerves, and take a step closer to the table.

"Everyone, this is my girl Elle. Ma, no questions. Don't scare her off." Everyone laughs at Vince and I pretend to laugh also. But fuck me, my nerves are shot.

"I'm so happy to meet you dear," Vince's mother, Linda, says. "Dante has filled me in on how you two met." I struggle to keep the smile plastered on my face. I'm certain there's a hint of truth in whatever he's told her.

"I'm a lucky girl," I say back as sweetly as possible. I may be scared and intimidated, but I want them to like me. Is that so wrong? If they like me, then maybe Vince will trust me more. Maybe he won't tie me up every single time he leaves the house. I wonder if I would leave though, if given the choice. Should I leave him? I'm not sure I would. Maybe I really am fucked up in the head.

"There's no doubt in my mind that he's the lucky one," Dom says to my left as Vince pulls out a chair for me. I smooth out my dress and take a seat.

"So, what do you do, Elle?" Becca asks. The swell of her pregnant belly touches the table even though she's leaning all the way back in her chair. I sure as fuck can't answer that question. What do I do? I do your brother-in-law. That's not an appropriate answer. Let's see, so far I've quit school, which essentially ended the career I've been busting my ass for years at. I don't have a job, and I'm not sure I'm going to get one. I've been painting which I love, and Vince thinks I should sell online. But I'm nowhere near confident in my work to even think about showing it to anyone. Not yet. Maybe someday.

I decide to circumvent the question and change the subject. "Oh my goodness! You look beautiful. Congratulations, you two." It's easy to compliment her. She really is radiant with her swollen tummy. "When are you due?" I ask to continue pushing the conversation along.

"Two months." Dom answers for Becca as he rubs her stomach. The look in his eyes is one of pure devotion. I find myself reaching for Vince's hand. I wonder if he'll look at me that way when I'm pregnant with his child. *If. If* I ever get pregnant with his child. Again, if I could run, maybe I would. I know I'm not pregnant now though. I just got my period before we came out for dinner. For some reason that hurts. Maybe I could justify staying with him if I was carrying his child, but I'm not.

"We're all so excited for another baby in the family," Linda says with a smile on her face. "Three grandbabies. I'd love a dozen of them!" Dante rolls his eyes, and Dom snorts.

"You'd better get on Clara and this one then," Becca points at me, "because after our little girl, I'm getting Dom fixed." The table roars with laughter, but my face heats with embarrassment and my fingers nervously tighten on Vince's hand. It's all too real.

"Damn, Becca, give them the chance to get to know one another before Vince has to knock her up," Anthony says, and grins at the two of us. I'm trying to relax, but just being around them has my fight or flight instincts on high alert.

Vince wraps his arm around my shoulder and kisses my cheek. He whispers in my ear, "Relax, sweetheart." His words instantly calm me. I close my eyes and take a deep breath. I don't care if it's sick. I can keep up this fantasy, whether it's right or wrong.

The conversation continues as two waiters bring large bowls of chicken alfredo and spaghetti with meatballs to the table. Ah. Family style. Becca licks her lips and reaches for the bowls, but can't quite get to them with her belly. I stifle a small laugh. It's pretty adorable watching her struggle. Dom smacks her hands away playfully and dishes out a large helping of both entrees onto her plate.

Tommy and Anthony start talking about bets and making wagers with Dom. Dante cracks a joke, and the entire mood seems to lighten and flow naturally. Laughter and chatter fill the air.

I start to relax into my seat, and think I can actually eat without feeling sick to my stomach with worry. When the tension finally leaves my shoulders, and just as I start to think I can do this, I hear a loud bang. And another and another, as glass shatters and people scream. I feel the air whiz by my head. I hear it over and over--a mix of screams and bangs. It's surreal.

Vince's hurls his body in front of me and pushes me out of my chair. I land hard on my back with his body caging me in. I look to my left and see Becca screaming and crying. Dom's holding and protecting her the same way as Vince is holding me. Tommy and Anthony are screaming at one another, but their voices are muffled. Each of them is down on one knee with their guns extended, propped up on the backs of the chairs for extra support. They're firing. Some of the bangs and bullets are coming from them.

"Get her out of here! Get them out!" I can barely hear Vince screaming as he lifts up my body. The sound of tires screeching echoes in my ears, and strong arms pull me away from Vince. I find myself running, my heart beating out of control as adrenaline races through my veins. My feet trip on a fallen chair and I land hard on the ground.

Dom doesn't give me a moment to right myself. Instead, he picks me up, tucking my body under his left arm, and carries me as though I weigh nothing.

"Vince!" I scream out as I see him jumping through the shattered large bay window. He doesn't stop. He doesn't hear me. He's gone and I'm being carried away.

I look around me behind the restaurant. It's a small alley. There are dumpsters at the end of it and the other side leads to the busy street. Dom is holding Becca, who's crying hysterically. No one else is here. I'm alone. I hear him shushing her. I hear the ambulance and the sirens from the police cars.

Reality hits me in the face. I can run. I can get the fuck out of here and save myself. I turn to look over my shoulder and Dom is staring me down. His face is all hard edges and his eyes hold an edge of a threat. But I doubt he'd leave his crying, pregnant wife to chase me down. But then again, I wouldn't get very far. I'm not a fast runner. I settle my back against the brick wall and sink down until my ass hits the pavement.

I feel far too sober. What the fuck am I doing? Who is this woman I've become? I wish Vince were here more than anything. I feel like that thought should be alarming to me. That it should send up red flags, but instead it offers me comfort. I'll feel better once he comes to get me. My gut twists. He better come get me. He better not get hurt. I don't know what I'd do without him.

The door to the right of me slams open, and Dante comes out. I rise to my feet and look behind him. Vince isn't there. My heart races faster. What if something happened to him?

"He'll be alright." I jump at Dante's words. He puts a hand on my shoulder, but I move away from him.

"This doesn't happen," I hear Becca say as she tries to calm her breathing. Her hand rests against her belly and she looks me in the eyes. "I don't know how long you've been with Vince, but I promise you this is *not* normal." She swallows and breathes in. She's sitting in Dom's lap and he's rubbing her shoulders.

This is not normal.

"Let's get you to the hospital, doll." He stands and helps lifts her up.

"I'm fine. I'm fine," she says, pushing him away. Dante walks closer to them, leaving me alone across the opposite side of the door.

"You should go to the hospital just to be sure. Get a look at my granddaughter and make sure everything's okay." He gives her a reassuring smile and Dom whispers something in her ear.

I can't handle this. I turn and walk to the door.

"I have to go to the bathroom." They all turn to me and I wait for a response. No one says anything. Both men look at me like they aren't sure I'm telling the truth. If I'm honest with myself, I'm not sure that I am.

"Make a right outside of the office," Becca answers with her eyes closed. I nod my head once, and walk through the door with my eyes on the ground. The commotion in the dining hall makes me walk faster. I get to the bathroom, shutting the door behind me and the noises are muted. It's quiet. I walk quickly to the faucet and turn it on. I take a moment to splash some cold water on my face, then run my wet hands down the back of my neck.

I breathe in and out. What am I doing? What am I going

to do? I swallow thickly. I don't know the answer to either question.

"Miss Hawthorne? Elle Hawthorne?" Hearing my name startles me and I turn around to face two women, each holding a badge out for me to see. It takes me a minute to realize what's going on. Two cops. Blood drains from my face and my hands go numb. Fuck. Fuck, this cannot be good.

"Yes?" I ask weakly.

"You're coming with us."

CHAPTER 28

VINCE

My feet pound against the pavement, my eyes focused on the red Honda ahead of me. Multiple car doors open and slam shut, then the tires squeal as they peel out. Someone fires a gun out of their window as I duck into Tommy's car.

He starts it and hits the gas. The tires spin, and my back presses against the seat as we take off after those fuckers.

They hit us on our home turf. With my mother there. My pregnant sister-in-law. My sweetheart on my arm. They're going to fucking pay for this shit.

"Don't lose 'em, Tommy!" I yell, leaning out of the window. I line up my gun and fire, aiming at the fucker in the passenger seat.

Bang! Bang! Bang! The third shot gets him. I see the asshole lean down in the seat and the driver turns the wheel but the motion is too sharp, and the car swerves into the intersection. They go over the lines and almost lose control of the car. We're closer now.

Tommy hits the gas, trying to get closer. But there are so many fucking cars out this late at night. My heart slams in my chest. They could've got my girl. Adrenaline fills my veins.

I look up and see we're closer. I need to get my head on right.

The driver keeps one hand on the steering wheel, then points his gun out of the window, spraying bullets. I duck behind the dash as a bullet hits the windshield. Tommy swerves, but stays on that fucker's ass. A car honks a warning, another to my right swerves to avoid us, and all hell breaks loose. A car behind us crashes into a parked car, and the traffic light turns red. Brakes squeal and my hands push against the dash.

Fuck! They speed through the intersection and several cars speed by us as they run the light. Tommy slams on the brakes, just barely avoiding a crash. Tires screech and the smell of burning rubber floods my lungs. My head slams down on the dash, and my palms push against the leather.

"Fuck!" I yell, slamming my fist into the dash. The cars finally start moving.

"Take me back. I need to get back to my girl," I tell him, feeling sick to my stomach. The fact that those bastards got away from me pisses me off. But I know who they are. And they're going to fucking die. Every last one of them.

Just as we park in front of the restaurant, my phone goes off.

"Vince." Dom sounds somber and I don't like his tone. My heartbeat slows and my vision seems to blur.

"Becca alright, Dom?" I ask first. I know my sweetheart's okay. I stayed with her until those cowards took off. I close my eyes and pray his baby's alright. I hate that I think the worst. But the way he said my name has my mind going crazy.

"She's alright."

"The baby?" I ask.

"She's good too. Got a good view of her sucking her thumb right now." I feel a little bit of relief at this. "Your girl..." He trails off, as if he's unsure how to say what comes next.

My heart skips a beat, and my lungs feel empty. That's what he called about. Elle. My sweetheart. She's okay. I know she is. She'd better be safe. I told him to take her. "What about her?"

"She's been picked up."

"No." I shake my head. No fucking way.

"We tracked her phone, Vince. And it was on the cameras. Two undercovers, not ours." I lean back against the side of the car. The sound of sirens is getting louder and louder, but I can't begin to process what that means.

"Vince, we gotta go!" Tommy's screaming in my ear, but his words barely register with me.

I look at him jumping in the driver's side as Dom talks away in my ear. I don't know what he's saying, and I don't care. I thought we had something. I thought she loved me. Loved what I did to her. Loved being mine.

The red and blue lights flash down the road ahead of us. They'll be here soon.

I turn off my phone and put a hand over Tommy's, stopping him from moving the car. We won't make it. They're gonna be here before we can get away. They'll see us. It'll be a chase. They don't have anything on us right now. Questioning. It's gotta be questioning about the shooting. *It's not my girl*, I say over and over in my head. *Not Elle*. This isn't about my sweetheart. My world feels like it's collapsing around me, but I refuse to believe it. There's been a mistake.

"Get out, and get low." I hand him the gun in my hand and push his shoulder toward the door of the car. Tommy doesn't waste a second, and I hop over the console to sit in his seat. As the cops roll up and park their car in front of mine, blocking me in, I get out of the car through the driver's side, making it appear as though it was opened for me. The fucking sirens and bright lights piss me off.

"Good evening, officers." I shut the door and walk to them as the uniformed men get out. Another car pulls up and Detective Anderson gets out. I narrow my eyes at him. I fucking hate that prick. He'd lie, cheat and steal to see us all behind bars.

"Vincent Valetti, you're under arrest."

My brows shoot up in surprise, but I don't fight them. It's foolish to put up a fight. That would just give them something they can actually charge you with. I mentally check off every possible thing in my head. No concealed weapons on me. Nothing they can pin on me. I can't think of a damn thing that they would be able to find in the car.

I try to breathe in and out calmly as I turn around and put my hands on my head. I know the drill. I lean my stomach against the car door. This isn't the first time it's happened. As they slam my head into the roof of the car, I see Tommy walking down the alley. He catches my eyes and nods. He knows the drill, too. My lawyer will be there faster than I will.

I'll be out in no time.

As long as this isn't about my girl.

CHAPTER 29

ELLE

"Elle, my baby!" My mother stands in the brightly lit front room of the police station. The place is mostly deserted, save for me, the two cops behind me and the one at the desk. And my mother.

I don't answer her. I don't know what to say. I'm still pissed off about how she dropped me from her life the second I had no money to give her. Her nose is bright red, and her eyes are watery. I'd say it's from crying, but it's not. She's drunk. I bite my bottom lip as the cops walk me closer to the front desk. They leave me standing there as my mother comes closer.

"Baby girl, are you alright?" she asks, with both hands

grasping for mine. *Baby girl?* My mother has never called me that. I pull my hands away from her.

"What did you do?" I snarl at her. She backs away slowly, looking to her left, then her right. Her hand comes up to her chest and if she were wearing a necklace she'd be clutching it.

"They called to tell me they found you," she answers.

"Found me?" I practically yell. "You knew where I was!"

"It's okay." She reaches out for me again. "We're going to get you out of this mess." I stare blankly at her as she continues. "I know he kidnapped you. I was so worried."

I sneer at her. "Were you worried when you called me a bitch for not giving you more money?"

She looks to her right and lowers her voice. "Just calm down. The police are going to give us a place out west. We're going to go into the witness protection program. Everything is going to be worked out. Just as long as you tell them whatever they need to know."

I look at my mother up and down. Does she think she's getting a fresh start? Is that what she sees this as? A get out of jail free card where her past mistakes vanish, and she can use this to her advantage?

"I love you. I really do." My voice cracks because it's true. I do love my mother, and for some reason it makes me sick. But I deserve better. I raise my voice and harden it. "I told you that you could call me. And you called once, for money. You really were 'so worried,' weren't you?"

"Elle." My mother tries to make her voice sound stern.

"You're drunk, mother. Go home and take care of yourself."

"I can't afford it on my own!" she yells at me. That's really what it all comes down to. It's always what it all comes down to.

"Then get a fucking job!" The officers come between us, and one pushes me toward the back, while a third comes behind my mother.

"You ungrateful bitch!" she screams at me as the officer pulls her away. She's drunk and being stupid and she tries smacking the officer away. I can't watch. She needs to get her shit together. I keep moving and try to ignore my mother's screams as the cops lead me to a back room. My heart fucking hurts. I can't help her if she doesn't want it though. I just can't put up with her shit anymore.

They open a door on the left and I walk through and almost laugh. It's just like the movies. A mirror and everything. I guess they're going to interrogate me. I choke on the ball forming in my throat.

At least they didn't handcuff me. I sit down and take a shaky breath. I'm not going to give them anything. Not a damn word. As soon as they close the door I say, "I want a lawyer."

"Miss Hawthorne. There's no need for a lawyer; we just want to ask you a few questions." My eyes dart to theirs. They have to give me a lawyer, don't they?

"I want a lawyer," I say without confidence. My heart beats louder in my chest. The weight of the situation comes down hard on my shoulders. I'm in the police station. Even if I don't say anything, they're going to know I was here. The *familia* will know. I close my eyes and for the first time in a long time I wonder if Vince will be able to save me.

If I don't say anything, they won't be mad at me, right? They can't blame me for being taken here against my will. I stand up quickly, and the chair tips over behind me. I look at each of them as though they've cornered me. "I want to leave!" My body heats, and anxiety overwhelms me. A man walks in. He's bald with bushy eyebrows, but he doesn't seem old. Maybe it's his broad build. His eyes are sharp, and his teeth are perfectly straight and white. He gives me a tight smile as he takes a seat across the table. He places his badge on the table.

"Hi there. Miss Hawthorne, I'm Detective Anderson, and I've been assigned to your case."

"Hello," I answer back.

"Try to calm down. We just have a few questions to ask, and then you can leave if you wish."

"We'd like to make you a deal," one of the female officers says. I forget her name. She told it to me, but I forgot. It all seems like a blur. The other woman picks up my chair and motions for me to sit. I sit down calmly and put my hands on my thighs. I stare at the table.

"We know you've been held against your will, Elle," the sweet blonde who looks about my age says. It's the first time she's really spoken. She sounds kind and she puts her hands out for me to hold, but I don't take it.

"I can't imagine everything you've been through. But we're here to help," she adds.

"We know you were abducted by Vincent Valetti on Sunday, May 16th." How do they know that? As if hearing my unspoken question, the blonde answers. "You were seen being forcefully pushed into the trunk of his car."

I feel shock first, then anger. I remember the unmarked white car I saw outside of my mother's place. They were watching me this entire time? Holy shit. They saw me being taken, and they did nothing!

"We need you to answer a few questions for us, and then we'll be able to give you a way out of this, Elle." I look at the man as he speaks. That's why. Bastards.

As I stare between the three of them, all I can think is that I wish Vince was here.

Rule two: I don't remember a damn thing, and I don't know what anyone is talking about. "I want a lawyer."

CHAPTER 30

VINCE

"We got you, Vince. You want to give us your story now? You got anything you wanna work with?" Detective Anderson sits back in his seat with a smug look on his face. I've been sitting here for a good half hour, just biding my time while they make me sweat it out.

I stare back at him with my mouth closed. I'm not saying a damn thing until my lawyer gets here. And then I'll be thanking them for their time and walking the hell out of here.

"Miss Hawthorne's already given her statement. You're going away for a long time Vince. The only way to ease up on your sentencing is to give us something. Something worth my while."

"Not saying a word." Cops will lie, cheat, and steal to get a statement. It hurts that she sold me out. But she's only got shit on me and no one else in the *familia*. And what do I care if I go away anyway? It's not gonna be the same, not after her. Not with her leaving me. My jaw tics and my fists clench. I wonder what she told them. I wanna know what my sweetheart really thought about me. About everything we went through together.

"She told us how you forced her into the trunk of your car and took her against her will." Fuck! I feel a sharp pain in my chest, like he fucking stabbed me. I can't believe she'd talk. Not my girl.

Even knowing she sold me out, I don't regret it. I love the way she made me feel. Even if everything that was real between us was only on my end. I can't stand the hurt in my chest. I fucking loved her. I still do. Tears prick at my eyes. I really thought she loved me. What a fucking idiot I was. I push down my emotions. They still aren't getting shit from me.

He's been babbling on with threats, but then he says something that rings clear in my ears. "She told us how you smacked her around and threatened her mother."

The tightness in my chest fades as his words sink in.

I smirk at them. Fucking liars. They were doing real good, too. I thought they had me. My girl wouldn't lie. I know she wouldn't. And I never said a word about her mother.

"You charging me with anything, officers?" I cock an eyebrow.

"We'll keep you in holding--" he starts threatening me, but I cut him off.

"And piss off my Pops as a result? How's that restraining order faring on your record, Detective Anderson?" He'd better not have upset Elle, either. She hasn't been through this shit before, so I can't imagine what she's feeling. "You better being treating my sweetheart good too. If you threaten her with anything, I'll make sure you lose your fucking badge."

Detective Anderson's nostrils flare with anger, and he slams his fist on the table. He takes off and slams the door on his way out. I know they'll keep me here for a bit longer. That's fine. So long as she's alright. My chest tightens with pain. The family knows she's here, but they don't know shit about her. A cold sweat breaks out on my forehead. I need to get to a phone. I need to get out of here. I start feeling fidgety, sitting in this chair. I've been at the station before, but I've never felt like this. Never felt the need to get the fuck out immediately. But knowing Elle will be out soon? Knowing they'll be waiting for her? I need to get out.

Chapter 31

Elle

I walk down the driveway with my arms crossed and my hands gripping onto my shoulders. I didn't have an address to tell them to drop me off at. I can't go back to my mother's, even if my name's on the mortgage, I don't want to be there. And I don't know Vince's address, even though I've been living there for the last two weeks. So I gave them the only address I had, which was Vince's parents' house.

I could run, I know that. I could go to a shelter and wait for the *familia* to eventually take me out. I could go into witness protection and give them everything I have on Vince. But I won't. I don't want to.

The blonde officer looked at me with pity, while the

brunette one like I was a fucking idiot. And maybe I am. I know I could go to a women's shelter. They tried to convince me that's where I should be while I get back on my feet. But that's not where I *want* to be. I want to be with Vince.

Dante opens the door with an aggressive look directed at the cop car. He looks pissed and it takes me by surprise, but it's not directed at me. Still, I struggle to breathe, and my gaze falls to the floor. Fuck, I knew I shouldn't have come here. This was a mistake.

I move to turn away and go anywhere other than here. I don't care where, but his strong hand comes down on my shoulder, stopping me from leaving. "Come on in," he says calmly. I look over my shoulder and see the female officers watching me. They look like they're waiting to pounce.

It's my last chance to decide. I know it is. I can go inside and risk whatever plan the *familia* has for me, or I can turn around and take my chances with the witness protection program. I look up at Dante and ask him the only thing I want to know. "Is Vince here?"

He gives me a tight smile as he answers, "Not yet." As soon as I hear his answer I walk inside quickly, pushing my body against the doorframe to get the fuck away from the cops. My arms are still wrapped tight around my shoulders.

"Elle!" Linda yells from the dining room. She strides toward me and wraps her arms around me. "Are you alright, sweetheart?" she asks me, pushing the hair out of my face. A soft smile forms on my lips. *Sweetheart.*

"I'm scared," I answer honestly. I really am. My body starts to tremble.

"It's okay, we've got you now." She pulls me in for a hug and gently pats my back. She doesn't understand that that's why I'm scared. I feel like a sheep that's walked into a lion's den. I open my eyes and see Anthony and Dante watching me closely, mumbling something to each other.

Dante walks toward us, and I pull away from Linda. I give her a tight smile as Dante tells her to go upstairs. She says something to him, a protest of sorts, but I can't hear. It's like white noise in my ears. I turn toward the window and look outside, only to see the cop car leaving, driving away to leave me to this fate I've chosen.

Dante stands next to me and puts a hand on my arm. "Come sit with me, Elle." I look up at him and try to speak, but I can't. The knot in my stomach grows larger and my skin turns to ice with fear. I nod since the words won't come out.

He leads me to his office. Anthony falls in line behind me. I'm convinced it's a sentencing. I'm being led to my death. Tears leak out of the corners of my eyes as I sit in the chair in front of his desk. Dante's quick to come to my side as I put my hands over my face and sob.

"I swear I didn't--" I try to speak, but a hiccup interrupts me.

He shushes me and pats my back. "It'll be alright, Elle. We're just waiting for Vince." Hearing his name helps calms me down.

Vince will take care of me. He'll protect me. I know he will.

After a moment my breath evens out, and my head seems to clear. I feel tired and emotionally drained as well. "When will he be here?" I finally manage to ask.

Dante searches my face for a moment, and I see Anthony sit in the chair on the far side of the room. "That depends on what you told them," he finally says.

"I didn't tell them anything," I answer back. A smile grows slowly on his face.

"I believe you." He sits at his desk and pulls out a bottle of some brown liquid. "Would you like a drink, Elle?"

I scrunch up my nose. "I don't like whiskey." He laughs from deep in his chest.

"Good thing this is bourbon then. I'm sure you could use a drink." He pours three shots, and gives one to me as Anthony reaches for his.

"Throw it back and I'll get you a chaser." He winks and tosses his shot back, so I do the same with mine. Ugh. It tastes awful.

I put the glass on the table and look at him straight in the eyes. "The chaser?" I ask. I could really fucking use it. I want to lick my dress to get this taste out of my mouth, but then I'd have to lift the hem up to my face, and that wouldn't be ladylike at all.

Before Dante can answer, the door opens behind me and I turn in my seat to see who it is.

"Vince!" I get up from the chair, knocking it into the desk and run into his arms. He holds me tight, and I melt into him. Everything is better now. I nuzzle into his arms. The heat from the liquor intensifies the warmth in my chest.

I pull back and look up at him with wide eyes. "I didn't--"

He kisses me on the lips, cutting me off. He pulls back and a small grin pulls at his lips. "I know, sweetheart."

"Do they have anything?" I hear Anthony ask.

"Nothing. They were reaching." Vince answers over the top of my head. He leans down and gives me a peck on the lips. I grip him tighter, and he rubs my back in soothing strokes.

"You did good, sweetheart. You did real good." Hearing his praise makes my heart feel light. He holds me for a moment and then they start talking behind me. I try not to listen as I shut my eyes and just focus on how good he feels.

"We need to get those MC bastards," Vince says, and it makes my eyes pop open. I want to ask who they are. I want to know if they were the ones who shot at us. But I remember the rules. I turn in his arms and look to the door. I'm afraid to ask if I can leave. I shouldn't be here listening. I know that much. But he pulls me into him, my back against his front, and he kisses my neck.

"We got 'em waiting for you, Vince." Anthony's eyes travel to my face and then back to Vince. "We figured you would want to do the honors."

"Damn right I want the honors. All of them?" he asks.

"Still looking for two of them." Anthony answers in a tight voice. It makes my stomach churn. Judging by the look on his face, that's really fucking bad. I try to ignore it all. I need to forget.

His hands grip my hips and he leans in to talk to me in my ear, "Sweetheart, you stay here."

I turn around and plead with him, "No. Don't leave me." I don't want him to go. I don't want to be left here.

"They put a hand on you, baby?" he asks me. "Who hurt you?"

I gently shake my head. No one's hurt me. "No one."

"That's 'cause you're mine." He kisses me on the lips. "I'll be back."

"Please, Vince. Just wait till I'm asleep. I need you." His face softens and he leans down to kiss me.

"I can do that, sweetheart."

"Good man," Dante says from behind me. "Take care of your girl, and then you guys take care of that shit tonight." Vince nods his head as Dante walks to the door and opens it. "Don't be late for dinner tomorrow," he adds before crossing through the door. Under his breath, he mumbles, "I gotta take care of your mother."

Vince smiles at his father and leads me to the door with his hand on the small of my back. "Let's go home, sweetheart. I'll take care of you."

CHAPTER 32

VINCE

Both men stare back at me. Only two out of four, but I'm giving them the full treatment. I want to send a message. These are the bastards who opened fire on me. On my family. On my sweetheart. My fists clench in anger. They're screaming through their gags. I wanted to make sure they were awake for what comes next. Tommy beat the shit out of one of them, and it was nearly 40 minutes before he woke up. It made it easier to tie his ass up to the truck though. The other one put up a fight, not that it was of much use against all of us. I stretch my jaw, feeling the slight bruise there from the shit punch he landed. I suppose if I knew I was going out, I'd fight like hell, too.

"Any last words?" I ask, knowing they're trying to say

something. I don't give a fuck though. They scream louder and fight the ropes that are chafing their skin.

"You ready, boss?" Anthony asks, as he tosses the container into the bed of the truck. It smacks against the one guy's leg and I swear to God he shits himself at the touch. The whole front yard of the Locos Diablos MC club house smells like gasoline, so I just take a few steps back. I hope the two fuckers we didn't find are in there right now or hiding somewhere watching. I want them to see this. I want them to know what's going to happen to them.

"Light it up." I don't turn my back as Tommy lights a match and tosses it at them.

I stare at the flames as they rise higher and higher. Their screams get louder and louder. I know the cops will be here soon, and I need to get my ass out of here. The smoke will rise and someone will call it in. I gotta get out of here in case it explodes, too. Everyone on the streets will know, though. You don't fuck with the Valettis. A chill runs through my body as I turn and get into the car. Tommy's in the driver's seat and Anthony's in the back.

"Am I taking you home, boss?"

"Yeah." I need to get home and feel her writhing under me. I'll need her every night until I die.

No one touches what's mine. No one but me.

CHAPTER 33

ELLE

I purse my lips as I look at the canvas. I set it up in the dining room so I'd get more natural light on it while I worked. There's just too much darkness. It's supposed to be a man's lips on a woman's neck, with his hand around her throat and her mouth parted. It was too realistic though, initially. I wanted to make it more abstract, so I added a black gradient to make them look like they were fading into it. But, I overdid it. I think I really fucked it up. I take a step back and put the brush on the easel as I take a deep breath in, and then out.

"They're going to love it, sweetheart," Vince says from behind me, and I smile. I keep my eyes closed as his arm wraps around my waist and he kisses my neck, just like I knew he would. He holds me to him and I open my eyes. We both stare at the painting.

"You think they'll really like it?" It's my first exhibit. The gallery next to Becca's restaurant is featuring me in their exhibit. I'm scared shitless. Painting is a lot of fun, and relaxing as well, but I never thought it'd be a viable career. There's so much risk and no stability. But Vince is right. It's the next step for me. It's been a few weeks since the shooting, and everything has finally calmed down. 've even gone out a few times with Becca. Vince didn't like the idea at first, since there's still something going on with the MCs, but he relented. I'm fairly certain him and Dom just sat outside of the restaurant every single time. I know they did at least once. Becca and I kinda of love it. How protective they are. The only place Vince has taken me is to family dinners and the gun range. I *need* to get out and do something. Thank God for Becca. I call her almost every day. She's going to pop sometime soon. Having her as a friend really helped me to take painting seriously. She calls me an artist, but I haven't earned that title yet.

My vow to be more social could be going better. I was going to take my mother to her AA meeting. But when I showed up and found her drunk and heard her excuses... I stormed off and haven't been back since. It wasn't worth cussing her out. I'm tired of putting the energy into helping her. I really do want to try; I want to help her. But I can't take her bullshit anymore.

I tilt my head and get a wave of inspiration as I look at the canvas. I need to make more of it black and white, and have the red lips saturated in comparison. That and more contrast on his hand. That would really make it pop.

"I've got it!" I yell out, and move to pick up the paints on the table.

"I gotta get going, Elle. Are you sure you wanna open those now? They'll dry up by the time I get back."

Arousal shoots from my chest down to my heated core. The thought of him leaving turns me on so damn much. He still ties me up when he leaves, and fucks me so fucking good when he gets back. I love it. I live for his touch. I clench my thighs and close my eyes trying to hide my desire. Not that it matters. He knows how depraved I am. And he loves it, too.

But playing during the daytime has waned a bit. I've been busy with shopping dates and luncheons. The women in his family are so friendly and open, I can't possibly say no to their invitations. He always ties me up at night though. And I fucking love it.

My eyes shoot open and I stare at the canvas. This is supposed to be done tonight, and it needs at least two days to dry completely. I bite the inside of my cheek contemplating what I should do.

"You need to get this done, don't you?" he asks, picking up his mug off the table. He grabs mine as well and walks to the sink.

"I really should," I say, as I take in more details of the painting. I should take advantage of this inspiration while I can.

"When I get back..." Vince walks over to me, and reaches under my nightgown to cup my pussy. He breathes on my neck and puts his lips up to my ear, "...you'd better be ready for me."

His words send a shiver down my back. My lips part and a small moan of lust escapes me. He turns me to face him and gives me a sweet kiss on the lips. I deepen it. I want him now. I always want him.

"Did you hear me, sweetheart?" he asks with a slight threat in his tone.

I look up at him through my thick lashes and place my hands on his chest. "Yes." I plant a chaste kiss on his lips. "I'll be waiting for you."

He smiles down at me. "That's my girl. I'll be gone for a few hours." He gives me another kiss, then gives my ass a squeeze before leaving me in the dining room.

I watch him as he leaves. I'm not sure what he's doing tonight. But I don't ask. He told me if anyone asks, that he plays the stock market. I sigh, feeling a little empty inside. I don't like lying, but luckily for me, no one has asked in the half a dozen times I've left this house.

I shake off the ill feelings and get to work. I add a little white paint, and then some black onto the easel. I need a really faint shade of grey though. As I dig though a mason jar of brushes for my favorite thin one, my phone goes off.

Becca. I grin from ear to ear. Baby time!

I answer the phone and have to refrain from asking if her

water broke. She told me she'd stab me if I asked one more time.

"Hello?" I answer in a playful, singsong voice.

"I need a trampoline," she says as clear as day on the phone.

"What?" A trampoline?

"I need to get this baby out! My fat ass needs to get on the trampoline and have gravity do its thing." I bust out laughing. I freaking love her. I smile as Rigs barrels into the room, wagging his tail that moves the back half of his body. He looks ridiculous. This dog is going to be huge when he's fully grown. I walk to the back door and let him out while she talks.

"I need to get this painting done and then have a nice glass of wine," I sigh into the phone as I shut the door, leaving him out to play in the fenced backyard. It's a large backyard. It's the perfect size for a trampoline or a swing set. I rub my belly, thinking we could have a little one someday. I could be complaining about heartburn and backaches like Becca does. I think I'd go with a swing set though. Trampolines seem a little scary for little ones.

"Well, have an extra one for me," Becca says with a laugh. I smile at Becca's playful tone, and then my heart stops.

I can hear Rigs snarling and growling, and then all of a sudden he's barking like crazy. My blood freezes, and my body goes numb with paralysis. I'm not okay. I turn to race to the backyard to get him. I need to get to Rigs. I don't make it two steps before the front door smashes open, and I scream and drop the phone. My body nearly falls to the ground, I just

HIS HOSTAGE 215

barely catch myself, and I cover my head with my arms before staring at them with wide eyes.

There are three or four men, all dressed in long-sleeved black shirts, wearing ski masks, covering their faces. One of them is pointing a gun at me as the others move around him, walking toward me with determined steps. One barks orders at the others. He sounds Hispanic. The responses he gets sound like American accents though. I try to pay attention to the details. I scream it out, hopeful that Becca will hear. "Four men! One is Hispanic! Gun! Al--"

A hand whips across my face, knocking me to the ground. A metallic taste fills my mouth. I see my phone on the ground. My heart sinks. It's off. It must've hung up when it fell from my hands. She didn't hear. My eyes close with failure. I know they're going to take me. I know there's nothing I can do. My body goes limp. I won't fight them. Not here. Not now. Not when I don't have a chance. I didn't just start living for them to come and kill me. It's not going to happen like this. I won't let it.

Someone kicks me in the stomach. I try to curl inward, but they grab me. The last thing I see is a fist coming at my face as one man holds my arms to my side and pins my back to his chest. The fists lands hard on my jaw, and the world fades to black.

I don't fight it. I'll wait.

And when I wake...

I will make them pay for taking me away from Vince.

CHAPTER 34

VINCE

I tap the small, black velvet box in my pocket as I get out of the car and shut the door. I can't wait to ask her. Well, I'm not going to ask. I'm going to tell her she's marrying me. It's been enough time that Ma will approve. She calls me after their lunch dates. I'm glad the two of them get along. Nothing at all like the relationship Elle has with her mother.

I cringe remembering how she reacted when I told her Sandra went to rehab. Maybe once she's out and stays sober Elle will believe she's changed. It seems like the more time she spends with the *familia*, the more resistant she is to forgiving Sandra. Which isn't necessarily a bad thing, it just hurts me thinking she won't have a relationship with her own mother.

My phone's going off again. I know it's Dom. He's been calling to get my ass down to the docks, but I told him yesterday, today, they would have to wait a while. Right now it's all for her.

I gotta pull the trigger on this. She deserves this for putting up with me. For fitting so perfectly into my life. That, and Ma will kill me if I don't put a ring on her finger before knocking her up. Part of me still thinks the *familia*'s waiting for her to run. But putting my baby inside her is gonna change all that for them. And this ring on her finger.

As soon as I see the door, I know something's off. Adrenaline pumps through my blood and my heart races. The door's cracked. It's been kicked in. The wood is splintered from where the door was locked. I always lock it behind me. Fuck. Fuck! I take the steps up slowly and pull out my gun. I want to call out for her. I need to know she's safe. But, I have to be smart.

I already fucking know who did this. I know it was Shadows MC. They're a bunch of fucking liars. They've been working with the Locos Diablos. They set them up to take the fall. But Tony got all their transfers and finances. I grind my teeth as I walk silently through the house. Rigs barks and paws at the back door. I walk to the dining room first. Two chairs are turned over and her canvas is on the ground. Broken. The paint is smeared on the tabletop. Her phone's on the floor.

Mine goes off in my pocket again and I answer it. I know

they're gone. Looking around the room, it's obvious they took her and ran. They want war.

I answer it and hold the phone to my ear.

"Vince! 'Bout fucking time! Becca's been--" Dom yells through the phone. I keep my eyes on the entrance to the dining room, just in case someone's here, hiding and waiting to jump me. But I know they're gone.

I cut him off. "They took her." I swallow the lump in my throat.

"Elle?" Dom asks after a quiet moment.

"Yeah." I bite back my emotions and let the anger come through. "Tony has their info?" I swallow the lump suffocating me and clear my throat. I put the phone back to my ear to hear him rattling off something in my ear.

"I don't want to risk going to the wrong place. We need to split it up."

"You sure that's smart, Vince? We could be outnumbered easily. They've got at least 10 of 'em at any given time at either the clubhouse or the warehouse."

"Well we'll have the advantage of coming up on 'em. They don't know that we're on to them. They have no fucking clue. But if we all show up to the wrong place, we're fucked. They'll know. They'll..." I don't say it. They'll kill her. I know they will. My chest pains and I struggle to take a breath. I can't even imagine what they're doing to her now. I don't want to think about it. But I can't help it. "I swear to God, Dom. I swear I'm gonna kill them."

"I know. I know," he says solemnly.

"I gotta go now. Text me the address."

"You need back up! Don't be stupid, Vince!" he yells back.

"Tell them to meet me there," I tell him. I can't wait. I won't.

"You won't do her any good if they kill you first." Fuck. I hate how right he is.

"I can't wait." I can't just stand here. She's most likely at one of those two places. And if she's not, someone there will know where she is. And I'll make them talk. I'll find her.

"I'm on my way. I'll call the guys now. I'll split 'em."

I nod my head. I can't talk. I try to, but my throat dries out and closes. If they killed her... If they put their hands on my sweetheart... I shake my head and focus on getting her back. I have to believe it's possible.

"Hurry up, Dom. And text me that address."

CHAPTER 35

ELLE

"We need to get her out of here." I wake up groggy, to a voice I don't recognize. My back is to them. I know they're behind me. I'm lying on my side, and I can feel a cool breeze on my face. I remain still and silent, and I'm sure to keep my breathing even. My face is killing me. My temples pound with pain. But I ignore the painful throbbing. I do a mental check. It's only my face and my side that hurt.

They didn't bind my wrists. I try to keep the smile off my face. Thank fuck they're behind me so they can't see my relief. Vince was wise to tie me up. These fuckers have underestimated me. My heart pounds in my chest, but I keep forcing myself to breathe evenly. I listen to them. I'll wait until

I can strike. I couldn't do anything back at the house, with all of them on me at once. I just need to wait until I have a chance.

I'm sure Vince will come. But right now, I can't rely on him. I don't know if he'll get to me in time. I also don't know how much time I have. I listen and wait.

"You really think this is going to work?" someone behind me asks. His voice is deep and throaty, like someone who's smoked his whole life.

"It's their signature move. They'll definitely believe it's a message from the cartel." Another man, one who's closer to me.

"They're a bunch of pussies." I can hear three men in total laugh. So I'm up against three of them. Those aren't good odds. I don't think I could take out three. My heart sinks. I won't give up hope though. I just need to try to take them on one at a time. I can manage that. I *will* manage that.

"Thought they'd have already gone after them. They move slow." My eyes slowly creep open as I continue to take stock of my situation. I'm facing a cinder block wall, lying atop cardboard boxes. My arm is above my head and it fucking hurts. I want to move it but I don't. I lie still and wait. Smoke fills my lungs with the smell of cigarettes and I hear a drag being taken.

"I want at her first." My eyes open wide, but I keep my breathing steady.

"You'll wait your turn."

"You sure they won't be able to get anything from the video?"

"Yeah, we'll edit it to cover our voices. It'll look just like the cartel's threats. Vince is a fucking stupid hothead. I know they'll go in for the kill as soon as it's sent."

The men laugh again, and I try to keep the sickness I'm feeling from creeping up my throat. But I can't. I nearly vomit at the image they've put in my head.

I'm fucked. I know it, too. A hand grips my hair and yanks my head back. I scream out with tears creeping out of the corners of my eyes.

"Our little bitch is up." I want to close my eyes, but I can't. A bald short man with yellow-stained teeth stares back at me with a menacing look. He's got a sick grin plastered on his face. From his voice, I recognize him as the one saying their plan will work. I decide to think of him as the planner in the group.

His nose is nearly an inch from mine and I take the opportunity to spit in his face. He wipes his face off with the back of his arm and then backhands me so hard I hit the cement ground with enough force that I nearly go unconscious.

"Get her ass up here." I hear him move around as I hear more heavy steps come from behind me. "We can all have a practice round." A sick, disgusting chuckle fills the hot air as I'm pulled up onto my feet. I turn around and kick the fucker as hard as I can right in his balls. The second hurls himself at me from my left side, and I ball my hands into fists, and draw back to punch him, but the first man's arms wrap around my front and hold me back. Fuck! No!

"No wonder he kept this cunt. I hope she fights us every time." A tall, thin man with oily black hair smiles and walks closer to me with his hands out to reach for me.

I don't care that I'm being held back. I'm not going to stop fighting. Vince would want me to fight. As soon as this bastard's close enough, I push my weight back and throw my legs up to kick him. The bald man holding me tilts backwards as he's knocked off balance, and my foot gets high enough to knock the guy square in the face. His head flies back as I fall to the ground and when I look up, blood's pouring from his nose. I don't waste a second, but the man behind me is faster. He wraps his arms around me and pins my arms in place. He holds me close and I'm trapped. I struggle against him, but I'm trapped in his hold.

The door to the room flies open.

"They're here!" A man barges into the room, completely out of breath.

"Who's here?" the bald fucker asks, his vile breath filling my nose and I try to push away from him again.

"Valettis!" the man yells, and the men all exchange quick glances.

"I'll tie her up. You three go now!"

They run out of the door and the bald man reaches into his jacket and I know what he's getting. I lunge at him. I'll pry it from his hands if I have to. I'll scratch, bite and claw. I latch onto his wrist while it's tucked at his side, gripping the gun, and sink my teeth into his arm as he fires a shot that hits the wall behind him.

He screams from the pain and pushes me away, but I bite harder, until his flesh rips from his arm and I spit it out, digging my nails and fingers into his arm and back.

The man looks down at me with a twisted snarl on his face and tries to shove me away. It gives me enough room to elbow him in his ribs and as he hunches over, the gun falls to the ground and goes off.

This is my chance. My only chance.

CHAPTER 36

VINCE

The tires screech and I jump out before we even come to a stop. I know they have cameras here. If there's anyone looking, they'll see us coming. I don't want to give them time to hide her. Or worse.

I hear Tommy and Anthony call out from my right as they each pull out their guns and run up to my side. Uncle Enzo and Pops are coming, too. Dom has Tony and Joey going with him. A few of the soldiers should be there waiting for them, too. Every last motherfucker is going to die.

I stand in front of the large doors and Anthony opens them up, staying behind the doors as a barrier. Not me. I'm planted right in front with my guns raised, one in each hand.

As soon as I see those fuckers I fire.

They don't even see it coming. Immediately I take out three MC assholes. Got one in the chest. Bang! Another in the head. Bang! Bang! Another tries to run, and I shoot that fucker in the back. Bang! Bang! Bang! I walk into the larger room. Stacks of coke and pot are on my left. Bricks of each of them, wrapped in plastic. A bagging station is on my right. Their operation is shit. And now, it's fucking over. As I walk in a gunshot goes off to my left and I fire. Bang! Bang! Bullets fly by me from my right. They whiz past me in what seems like slow motion. Anthony gets a kill. Another MC fucker in leather drops behind a counter. He was counting the cash. With the doors open the wind blows the money off the table.

I walk over to the fucker who got a shot off. Looks like a gunshot caught him in the neck. It must've hit an artery, judging by the way blood gushes out from the wound as his heart pumps. He's clutching the wound with both hands as blood pools around his head and soaks his hair. His eyes focus on me. He tries to speak, but blood coughs up his mouth. I point the gun at his head and pull the trigger.

I keep walking at a fast pace with my guns raised. My heart beats frantically, trying to jump out of my throat and the only sound I can hear is the blood rushing in my ears. But on the surface, I'm a cold-blooded killer, walking with purpose, moving with a deadly calmness that would frighten sociopaths. I have one goal in mind. Only one thing that matters.

My girl. My sweetheart.

Three men run out with guns firing, and a bullet hits me right in the chest. I fire off both guns. One man's downed immediately but the other two move off to the side to take cover behind an old rusted car. Tommy and Anthony go up the right side and duck as the guns come up and fire aimlessly. I take a step forward and aim. I hit the hood right where the hand was and hear the bastard swear. That's not good enough. If he's talking; he's breathing. I walk forward and watch my guys go up the right side, sneaking behind. I'll distract them. I run up close and fire continuously. Four more shells each. Bang! Bang! Bang! Bang! They sound off one after another, after another, until I'm firing blanks. I keep pulling the trigger, letting the empty clicks fill the air. I want them to know I'm empty. I'm counting on them to stand up and fire at me. And they do. As soon as they're visible, shots fire from behind them and both men only get a single shot off. One just misses me. But the other lands on my chest, close to the first shot that hit me.

It hurts like hell.

I look down and make sure the Kevlar held up and there's no blood. I'll fucking live. But not without my girl. I take the pain and keep moving as I reload my guns. I need to find her.

I know there are rooms in the back. She's got to be in one of them. My phone's in my pocket. It's silent. I don't know how they're doing at the clubhouse. But until it goes off, I've got to assume she's here. My eyes raise and my guns point at a door as I hear bullets firing in the distance, somewhere in the back, and a terrifying scream.

Elle!

All at once we run down the hall, my only focus on the door. I need to get to her. She's here. I heard her.

Gunshots fire over and over. Three shots, four shots, five shots. No!

I kick the door and it flies open. I run through ready to fire, and instead I stand in shock.

Anthony and Tommy stop behind me. I hear Uncle Enzo yell something from the back, but I don't know what. All my focus is on my girl.

She's got blood on her face. A nasty bruise on her chin. And she standing, breathing heavy, with her arms straight, holding a small gun. It's pointed down at a short, bald man lying face down on the floor. His leather jacket is speckled with bullet holes and blood. So much blood, pooling around his body.

"Elle," I call out to her, and lower my guns. I see Anthony and Tommy searching the room. I hear a yell clear outside the room, it sounds like Pops. But I'm not paying attention like I should. I walk to my girl. She hasn't moved, except for her chest rising and falling with each heavy breath as she keeps the gun still pointed at the dead man.

"Sweetheart?" I try to get her attention, and it works. Her startled eyes find mine, and her body relaxes finally. She drops the gun to the ground. It falls to the cement floor with a loud clank and she runs to my arms.

Her small body wraps around me and she holds onto me tight. I hold her to me, loving how she's clinging to me. But hating that she had to do this. Hating that she went through this.

"Are you alright, sweetheart?" I finally ask her. She doesn't pull away and doesn't answer.

"We gotta go, Vince," Tommy says to my left. I turn, still holding her to me and see all the guys looking at us. I nod my head and kiss her hair.

"Sweetheart, are you alright?" I ask again. My heart won't beat right until I hear her talk. I know it won't. I just need to hear her say it. I need to hear her voice to really believe I'm holding her in my arms.

She nods her head in my chest and pulls back. Tears run down her face. "I'm okay," she answers me, and then wipes her face. My lips crush hers in a passionate kiss. Her hand wraps around my neck and she kisses me back with the same ferocity.

"I was so scared, Vince," she whispers with her eyes closed as she pulls away.

I kiss the tip of her nose. "I got you now, sweetheart."

She hugs me close, molded to my side, as we walk over the dead body and leave the room. "I won't let that happen again. I promise you," I murmur into her ear. I see my men nod and walk around us. They've got us covered so I can just hold her and give her the comfort she needs.

She looks up at me with tears in her eyes. "You'd better not." She gives me a small laugh, but it's accompanied with tears.

"I promise you, baby. No one's ever going to hurt you again." She buries her head in my chest and wipes her face on my shirt before looking back up at me. I wait until her eyes are firmly on me. "I love you."

"I love you too, Vince." She reaches up to kiss me again as we exit the warehouse and I have to stop to wrap my arms around her and kiss her back. "I love you so fucking much."

Epilogue

Elle

"You look beautiful." Vince's mom mouths at me as I walk down the aisle of the church. I smile at her and mouth back a thank you. The church is gorgeous. It's more beautiful than anything I've ever imagined. St. Rose. The family church. The large stained glass windows and intricate frescoes on the walls give it an old-world feel. It's a traditional wedding, during Sunday mass. So I don't know everyone, but all eyes are on me.

My hands tremble and I hold the bouquet tighter. I love my wedding dress. It has a sweetheart neckline, with an A-line silhouette and it's covered in expensive lace. The gown hugs my baby bump and my curves before flaring out at the top of my thighs. My eyes focus straight ahead. Vince is waiting for me. His hair is styled neatly and he's clean-shaven. His suit is perfectly fitted to his muscular form, and emphasizes his broad shoulders. His eyes travel down my body with lust, and I find myself walking faster. I have to really work to slow my walking to match the pace of the bridal chorus.

Everyone's here. Even my mother came. She's in the back, and I'm not sure if she'll speak to me, but it's a start.

I take a step up the stairs and feel my heart swell with happiness. It overrides my nerves and I take another, to stand with him in the center of the room in front of everyone.

"You look beautiful, sweetheart," Vince says, as I turn and pass the bouquet to Clara. I feel my cheeks heat with a blush. Behind Clara, Becca's holding her little girl. I insisted she still stand up here as my bridesmaid, even if Cloe was being a little Velcro baby. My heart swells and tears prick at my eyes.

I can't wait for the vows, or any of the readings. I'm so overwhelmed with emotion.

"I love you, Vince." I lean forward and give him a quick peck on the lips.

Vince smirks at my impatience. His hand wraps around the back of my head and the other around my waist and he pulls me in for a kiss. A real fucking kiss. My lips mold to his and my body bows under his touch. The cheers and catcalls from the members of the church make me wanna pull away, but I know better.

"Alright, alright, you two," the priest says, and Vince

finally loosens his grip on me. I know my cheeks are bright red and I'm slightly embarrassed, but Vince takes my chin between his thumb and his forefinger and makes me look him in the eyes. I'm lost in his look of pure devotion.

About the Author

Thank you so much for reading my romances. I'm just a stay at home Mom and an avid reader turned Author and I couldn't be happier.

I hope you love my books as much as I do!

More by Willow Winters
www.willowwinterswrites.com/books